D1682561

SPLAT! SPLAT! SPLASH!

The windshield was a mass of brown and green. Vision was impossible through the thick layers of insect crud. Carl Barks stopped the car and got out to clean them off.

Then he saw them converging upon him, their dark bodies blending together like some portentous shadow. His eyes grew wide as he realized the true horror — beetles whose crusty bodies were now showing in the moonlight. He caught a brief glimpse of Karen through the partly cleaned windshield and saw the terror on her face. Then he bolted for the driver's door and grasped the handle.

He gasped. The handle was a mass of living, biting beetles. They were on his hand, ripping at his flesh, causing a flow of bubbling scarlet. . . .

bugged!

DONALD F. GLUT

MANOR
BOOKS
INC.

A MANOR BOOK 1974

Manor Books Inc.
329 Fifth Avenue
New York, New York 10016

Copyright, ©, 1974, by Manor Books Inc.
All rights reserved. Published by
arrangement with the author.
Printed in the U.S.A.

bugged!

CHAPTER ONE

Cincidella waited.

For what he waited, Cincidella did not know. Still, the knowledge would come to him as it had before. And this time the thing for which he waited would be different.

The world was dark that night. Shadows crawled and spread about the looming foliage. The world was peaceful, especially so, as if some ethereal serenity had settled with the twisting evening mists.

The only light beamed from the full moon, glowing ivory from the black sea that roofed the world. The luminous globe bathed Cincidella in its light, accentuating the yellow squiggles that interrupted the monotony of his dark green body.

Cincidella raised his head. He looked up at the moon and was awed by the splendor and majesty of its fullness.

He moved slowly on six hairy legs. As he had done so often in the past, Cincidella moved his filamentlike antennae, as if to reach the circular deity. But then he knew that this was not the time for such seemingly impossible attempts at unattainable goals.

Now was the time of that inexplicable craving. The craving that was so contrary to the Way.

This was the night of the Call.

The Call had come from some unseen and unknown god or demon. But the origin of the Call did not matter in this world of warmth and wetness and darkness. That the Call existed sufficed, and with the Call came the craving.

Cincidella experienced the hunger. The hunger gnawed at him as though he were the consumed rather than the consumer. And though the hunger revolted him, he knew it must be satisfied.

The moment for which Cincidella waited had not yet arrived. But he knew that the moment of satisfaction could not be delayed much longer. This pleased Cincidella, for the hunger was gradually becoming torturous. He loathed the Call for imposing that craving, but also appreciated its providing the means for satisfaction.

Cincidella's antennae vibrated. His head turned toward the junglelike flora that somehow lessened the moon's brilliance. Jerkily, the antennae wiggled, signaling.

The shadows lived. They crept through the thick growth of vegetation as the Brethren slowly came into the clearing. Now their bodies, too, received the cool spray of moonlight. The colorful designs of their greenish backs—yellow gold—glowed in the moonlight. But their radiance was not as brilliant as Cincidella's.

Cincidella was leader to the Brethren. Following the Way, they responded to his summons. They could readily detect his drifting signal with its implicit message. This night, however, their response was not merely to his signal, but more to that greater force which had lured them from their dark haunts.

The Call.

Cincidella stood motionless as the Brethren approached. They numbered in the thousands. Slowly they surrounded him in a dense circle of pulsating life. They were waiting. And though they were now creatures of the Call, they awaited some command from their leader, some signal which would inform them as to why they hungered.

The leader walked toward the inner rim of the living circle where it parted, creating a pathway through which Cincidella passed with regal poise.

When he had completely passed out of the circle, the Brethren regrouped. His minions then followed in disorganized formation, moving as though weightless across the dampness of the earth.

They halted at the edge of the world.

Cincidella extended his right foreleg. He touched the vast smooth expanse of whiteness that stretched in two directions and was swallowed by the distant blackness.

Wisps of nighttime fog became diaphanous clouds that settled upon the smooth ribbon that bordered the world. The moon cast bluish halos upon that white strip, and elsewhere there was only darkness.

The leader knew that waiting was nearly at an end. His head swiveled, eyes looking down the ribbon to where he knew there was no world.

And then Cincidella saw . . .

Eyes.

Two gleaming eyes, faint in the distant blackness. The eyes of some terrible dragon, the type which Cincidella and the Brethren had often perceived thundering along the edge of the world.

The Call would soon provide for them. But first there were others, not of the Brethren but similar in nature and purpose, to respond to this great demon-eyed monster.

Splat!

Howard Barks had been watching the images that flew behind him as his brand new Ford Fairlane maintained 25 mile per hour speed along the poorly paved road. The images had a strange unearthly beauty, the way they shimmered in the light of the full moon. The bog was magnificent in its raw and unspoiled splendor. But now Barks' eyes naturally focused upon the wet brown smear that streaked the windshield of his automobile on this Friday night.

"Damn!" exclaimed Howard Barks, grinding his teeth. "Damn those bugs!"

The young woman seated beside him smiled.

"Temper, temper, Dad," she said. Her golden-blonde hair streamed with the warm air blowing through the open window at her right. The rush of air filled the car with the odors of the bog, smells of lush vegetation and unseen animal life.

"It always happens this way, doesn't it, Karen?" Howard Barks continued. There was a scowl on his face which caused his neatly trimmed gray mustache to curl upwards on the left side. His smooth fingers, callus-free from two decades of executive work with the manufacture of photographic equipment, gripped the felt-covered steering wheel. "You get the car washed in the afternoon on the way home from work. And before you can even get where you're going, what happens? Either rain or bird turd or some God-damned bug always messes up your windshield. It's always the same."

Karen, with large chestnut eyes, looked over at her father.

"I dislike insects as much as you do," she said. "But if you'll stop complaining, I promise to get out the Windex and a fresh new jar of elbow grease soon as we get back home. Deal?"

"Well—"

"Come on, now. Don't bother with one silly bug. Get your mind back on the reunion."

The frown on Barks' face metamorphosed into a smile. His thoughts were gradually pulling away from his insect-marred windshield and returning to the reason for his driving through this desolate area. Suddenly he felt a glow of nostalgia.

"You know," he said, "I really feel kind of strange about going to this reunion. In a way I feel as young as when I was back in college."

"You and your fraternity brothers were really close then, weren't you?" she asked.

"Thick as thieves, as we used to say in those days. Our frat was made up of the school elite. Hmmm . . . I wonder what the rest of the fellows will be like. After all, it's been twenty-five years."

"Probably a little fatter, a little less hair. Just like you, Dad."

"You're probably right," he replied with a smile. "You know, I'm actually excited. I wonder if we'll still have anything in common after so many years. You know, I'll never forget the thrill of opening that envelope and finding the invitation inside."

Karen looked toward the open window. She let the wind rush against her pretty face. Her hair flew about wildly.

The moon seemed to run alongside the car as it continued at modest speed along the road. Cold light spilled from the open spaces in that lush shadow-crossed flora, creating moonbursts that imparted beauty to the otherwise dismal swampland. A ribbon of rippling silver broke the dark surface of the river. The slow-moving water was visible through the white spruce and cedar trees that grew profusely in the bog.

The girl shrugged her shoulders.

"But why out here?" she inquired with the sound of perplexity in her melodious voice. "Of all places for a reunion, why did your frat pick Desolation Row?"

Barks considered her question for a few moments before answering.

"Probably because Ronald Reid thought up the idea for a silver anniversary reunion," he said.

"Ronald Reid? I remember you mentioning some members of the old frat before, but never anyone named Reid."

"Reid—or Dr. Reid as he's now known—was never the most popular member of our group. I guess we were all oddballs back then, but Reid took the cake. I suppose that's why he eventually bought a house out here in the swamp after he quit school."

"If I'd known we'd be going this far out into the sticks, I'd probably have stayed home. Besides, I still don't think I'll fit in tonight. You and your friends will want to talk about old times and old girlfriends and won't want some dumb 21-year-old sitting around like an extra piece of furniture."

"Nonsense," said Barks. "You're an intelligent girl, Karen, and will probably make some excellent contributions to the conversation in case we run out of old times or old girlfriends to talk about. Anyway, you had nothing to do tonight and I hated to see you bored again." Looking at his daughter, he saw her smile begin to fade.

Before this the bog had been strangely silent. But now the swamp was coming alive with unidentifiable noises. There were sounds that might have been the chirps or shrieks of some hungry night bird. Or something else.

Barks frowned. His shoulders wriggled beneath his tweed suit. The noises of the swamp, of the night, were making him feel uneasy.

"Probably more of those damned insects," he grumbled. "Listen to them chatter. You'd think they were having a bug convention or something out there.''

The steady commotion emanating from the moonlit bog seemed to compete with the purring sound of the car. But eventually there was no more contest. The noises made by the insects reigned supreme.

''They sound like they're out there waiting for us, don't they?'' said Barks.

''Oh, Dad!''

''Sorry. Guess I'm still mad about that windshield. Aw, let them chirp all they want. Just as long as they don't mess up my car anymore.''

Splat!

''What the hell—? Another one!''

Splat!

Splat! Splat!

Howard Barks gasped. He looked straight ahead.

Karen was moving close to him. She grasped his right arm, almost jerking it from the steering wheel.

''Karen, please—'' he began.

The impact with which the insects splattered themselves against the windshield seemed almost forceful enough to break the glass. There was now an explosion of the tiny creatures, appearing in the hundreds . . . thousands . . . all squashing their brittle exoskeletons against the tinted glass.

''Shit!'' Howard Barks erupted. ''They're acting like some God-damned *kamikaze* pilots. Like they're attacking the car! Trying to smash through the windshield with their bodies!''

''Dad . . .''

''Shut up, Karen! Got to think. Figure out what the hell's going on!''

The Fairlane swerved beneath the relentless bombardment of insects. The windshield dripped with the gore of the creatures. The sounds of insects shrieking and chirruping was maddeningly loud. The once-black finish of the car was now caked with smears of chitinous bodies and internal fluids.

Barks thought of Karen. Considered the danger.

"Karen, roll up the windows! All of them! Before they can get inside the car!"

Karen did as she was told, but barely in time. The insects were now attacking the car from the sides.

Splash!

She jerked from one end of the seat to another.

The windshield was a mass of brown and green. Vision was impossible through the thick layers of insect crud. At last the scum-encrusted vehicle halted alongside the road. Its tires sank several inches into the spongy ground.

Barks muttered something inaudible, then let himself fall against the steering wheel.

"There's no sense in going any further," he complained. "I can't see a thing through that windshield and I'm not going to move this car until I can."

He waited.

Then, unpredictably, the insect siege stopped. The swamp was quiet again save for the lingering sounds of night. From somewhere in the distance came the welcome hooting of an owl.

Howard Barks did not comprehend the nature of what had happened. But he prayed the danger had gone. For several minutes the quiet continued. He gripped Karen's hand firmly and felt her sweating.

"I think it's all over," he told her. "I don't know what happened out there. But whatever it is, thank God it's over."

Karen reacted. Her large brown eyes seemed to grow larger. Tightly she clasped her father's hand.

"But if those bugs attacked once," she said, "there's no guarantee they won't do it again."

"I realize we've been through an experience. But what happened out there had to be a fluke. Something for Ripley's *Believe it or Not!* It's like lightning not striking twice in the same spot. Now I don't know about you, but I want to get the hell away from here and over to Reid's place, where I can relax with a stiff drink and try to forget all this."

He started to open the car door when Karen grabbed his arm and said, "No, Dad."

"It's all right, I tell you. All I'm going to do out there is clean off those windows so we can see again."

Without another word, Howard Barks leaned to the right and took a clean rag from the glove compartment. Then he stepped outside and began to clean the sludge from the windshield.

Cincidella observed the dark shadowy shape through his compound eyes which provided him with excellent vision, better than that of his brothers.

The shape was like some sleek black mountain.

But Cincidella knew that this was but one of the many fire-eyed dragons who often roared along the edge of the world. He also knew that the time of waiting had ended.

Standing beside the dragon was a monster of incredible size and hideous appearance. Its heat allowed Cincidella to see it clearly. The enormous forelimbs blurred as they waved over the great dragon's brow.

The antennae of Cincidella's head wavered, and the Brethren mimicked the action of their leader. They knew that this was the time for fulfillment. The time to move.

Cincidella, the tiger beetle, would marshal his six-legged brothers against the laws of the Way and in accordance with the Call.

The beetles had all turned to face their shadowy adversary.

Boldly Cincidella conducted them. For truly he was the fiercest predator of them all. And while Cincidella assumed his position of authority over his minions, the shadowed monster stood before the flaming eyes of the dragon.

Howard Barks felt his shoes sinking into the soggy marl. The odors of the bog were strong, forcing him to breathe through his mouth to avoid them. He paused, looking down at the muck that enveloped his shoes. For a short while he pondered the various ingredients—the shells, the clays, the carbonates of magnesium and calcium—that formed what served as earth. He lifted one foot though the marl and peat held tenaciously to the soles of his brown shoes.

He proceeded to wipe the windshield. The cotton rag became more and more caked with the compounded remains of the insects with his every sweep. The odor was offensive to him. If only he could be smelling the laurel or cotton grass which grew in abundance in the bog.

Then Howard Barks heard them.

Again.

God! he thought. The insects couldn't have returned. That was a crazy thought to entertain and a thought that made his spine feel like ice. It was impossible for the insects to return for a second attack, singling out this one representative of the world of *homo sapiens*. Impossible. For that would imply something like premeditated murder and—

But no, he did hear them. Insects. Their noise becoming louder, louder, much as it had just previous to smashing against his car.

He turned and his heart nearly ruptured.

The sounds were behind him, to his sides. They issued from every possible direction. Everywhere.

Then he saw them, moving toward him as swiftly as their miniscule legs permitted. They were converging upon him, their dark bodies blending together like some portentous shadow.

Barks' eyes grew wide as he realized the true horror of these creatures—beetles whose crusty bodies were now showing colorfully in the moonlight. He *had* been singled out! He caught a brief glimpse of Karen through the partly-cleaned windshield. He saw the terror on her face. Then he bolted for the driver's door and grasped the metal handle.

Metal? He gasped.

The handle was a mass of living, biting beetles. They were on his hand in moments, following its contours and assuming its shape. And they began to rip at his flesh, sharp mandibles pinching and causing a flow of bubbling scarlet.

Barks screamed in agony. Instinctively, he smashed his hand against the insect-coated fender of the car. But even as his hand became wet with the juices that spilled from the cracking insect bodies, he felt his legs attacked by more of the creatures.

He stumbled backwards. His feet trampled a hundred of the creeping horrors, crunching them into oblivion as he fell against the spongy ground.

But the loss of a hundred insects did not lessen the attack. Relentlessly they continued to besiege this man who had invaded their world. Tiny legs ascended Barks' legs beneath the coarse trousers. Crimson flowed from the ever increasing number of wounds, soaking the tweed fabric of his pants.

Barks lashed out at the beetles, his arms flailing.

But the booming beetles returned in droves. And every one of those biting monsters seemed intent on one hideous mission —tearing Howard Barks to shreds!

Truth exploded in Barks' mind. *God! they're eating me. Eating me alive! If I could make it to the car—*

But flight to the Fairlane was insane. Impossible. The car was already thick with the dead monsters. And besides, Karen was there. He wasn't about to have her open that door and become a meal for the beetles as he was now. There was only one possible escape and he knew it. Yet, there were only seconds left to put his plan into operation. Already the beetles were crawling up his body. About his stomach and chest. His arms.

Now his neck.

Consuming!

The river! he thought. He tried to shake the clinging insects from his arms. *The river!* Already the thousands of pains were fusing into one. *If I can only get to the river—* His body jerked spasmodically. He staggered to weakened feet. *If I can get to the river, maybe I can drown the filthy little bastards!*

As he struggled to walk his feet stumbled over the crumbling sphagnum. His heels trampled sundew and pitcher plants. His body cut black spaces in the curling mists. And from behind, through the incessant noises of the insects of the bog, he thought he heard Karen's voice calling him.

Through the biting haze that covered his face, he saw her. She was bolting from the car, seemingly unconcerned about her own safety. Her feet sank deep into the soft ground as she ran. Her legs moved swiftly beneath the hem of her short blue dress. Within seconds she was beside him, gaping incredulously at him, pondering what on earth she could do.

She said nothing, but searching frantically she finally found a yard-long branch of wood. Then she began to hack away at the creatures. But her blows only inflicted more pain upon her now blood-soaked father.

The river shimmered in the moonlight. It was visible between the black spruce trees. The river seemed to beckon to him, offering a release from pain.

With supreme effort, Barks trudged toward the bank. He felt his strength flowing out of him along with the streams of blood. With what remained of his strength, he collapsed falling face down into the stinking, slimy water.

Scum and water flooded his mouth. He tasted putrescence. He turned onto his back and moonlight flooded his eyes. Still he struggled, half submerged and trying to shake the tiny predators. Again he moved, this time into a position that allowed him to see the surface of the river. The cold water in his mouth prevented him from screaming. Yet, he so wanted to scream.

More beetles approached. Beetles that were different from the others. Aquatic beetles.

They crawled from the water and up his face. Into his mouth. His eyes. They too inflicted their bites. They too began to eat, feeding upon his distended tongue. Barks could taste the blood in his mouth. The blood and the beetles.

Agony, more excrutiating than before, attacked his right hand. And when Barks lifted it with painstaking effort he saw the gleaming white hand of a skeleton. But the sight was brief for, moments later, he no longer had eyes to see.

Then mercifully, Howard Barks slipped into oblivion to further feed the horde of hungry beetles.

Cincidella was the last of his kind to feast. Why he hungered, he did not know. But hunger he did and feast he must.

Swiftly he climbed the corpse that had lured his aquatic brothers to the banquet. His large eyes found raw meat and blood. Though this was not the Way and though he preferred the sustenance afforded by the bodies of other insects, Cincidella ate.

Cincidella feasted to his capacity. Even when he had filled himself, he continued to bite and discard the flesh. When he had grown too weary to continue, he permitted the other beetles, who still hungered, to satiate themselves upon the giant kill. As the last of the desired shreds of flesh passed from the grinning thing that gleamed white in the moonbeams, Cincidella led the Brethren away from the river. Then they all stopped.

There was still the second creature. This one was almost as gigantic as the first. It stood motionless before Cincidella and his followers as though planning some mode of attack.

Cincidella trained his antennae upon the light-colored shape and saw the golden tendrils. For several moments he wondered if he should attack once more.

But there was no hunger. No signal from the Call. No command to continue the attack.

Thus Cincidella left this second creature. And as he led his hordes back to the concealing shadows, the bog returned again to peace.

CHAPTER TWO

Karen Barks did not remember how long she screamed and cried. For how many minutes or hours she wept, she neither knew nor cared. For crying was reality and reality was a thing she wished to forget. Reality was the witnessing of her father struggling helplessly, writhing from what must have been the most excrutiating of agonies, as his flesh was eaten away by ravenous insects. Yet reality was inescapable. Now the horror had ended and that was all that mattered.

Ended?

The horror?

Her thoughts swirled. Desperately she tried to compose herself, for there was a shape—a moving shadow approaching. Karen blinked her eyes, washing them with tears. Then she focused upon the distant figure that came toward her.

A giant, clad in a soiled and worn butler's uniform, stalked the mist-enshrouded swampland. Under his weight, his oversized and unpolished black shoes squished through the soggy ground. His stride was steady, heavy, hardly affected by the sucking matter underfoot. There was a determination in his gait as if he were entirely familiar with this dismal area.

Insects were stridulating, insects so numerous in variety that their noises blended into one omnipresent undulation. The boom of beetles; the creaks and chirrups of crickets; the pipes of myriad other species of hexapod life that infested the swamp—all sounding as one. Yet the giant seemed not to notice.

Karen stood several yards away from the insect-smeared car. The air about her was warm, muggy, while the mists that enveloped her legs provided a deathly chill. Her back was to the river, her long hair blowing in the breeze. She was still crying. Only the steady sound of his feet sloshing through soggy ground and the foreboding appearance of the approaching figure held her attention.

The black-attired giant broke the wisping trails of mist that snaked between the balsam and white cedar trees. He seemed to be some awesome apparition of the bog. There was no expression on his rather cruel-looking face. His gray hair was unkempt while bushy gray speckled eyebrows met above his aquiline and obviously once-broken nose.

And as the figure steadily advanced, Karen swore that he was nearly seven feet tall.

The giant stopped some fifty feet away from her. His eyes glinted as he inspected her from top to bottom. Yellow teeth were revealed as he finally showed some expression on his face—a smile that should never have been.

Karen could feel those eyes as their cold gaze crawled about her. She wore a particularly short dress that evening, the same dress she had worn a month ago when she modeled fashions for a chain of department stores. The dress accentuated her long, well-shaped legs and clung to her so there could be no doubting the trim waist, the fullness of her breasts. She could feel the wind causing the hem to flutter.

As the giant's grin grew wider, Karen felt all warmth suddenly dissipate from the muggy atmosphere of the swamp. She winced. Self-consciously she stepped backwards, sinking several inches into the oozing ground. As if witnessing her father's death were not enough for this night, she had now to contend with some gigantic pervert who had lumbered out of the shadows of a swamp for God-only-knows what degenerate pleasures. But perhaps the giant would merely kill her, quickly, compassionately. After what she had already seen, whether she lived or perished didn't matter.

Raising a hand that could have belonged to a professional wrestler instead of someone dressed like a butler, the giant spoke.

"Sorry I scared you," he said with a gutteral voice that sounded like a claw grating over gravel. The giant looked toward the Fairlane with its coating of dead insects. The headlights were still beaming, however dimly, through the muck. "But I saw the lights on your car and thought you might be in a jam. Lots of folks get stuck out here, you know. Lots of 'em get stuck and never come back."

Taking a step forward, the giant closed the gap between them by over a yard. His proximity to Karen was unnerving. There was a feeling akin to an electric charge rising up her spine. The moonlight bathed his swarthy skin in a bluish glow and added to the unsightliness of his features.

"Who are you?" he asked. "And what are you doing out here alone?"

Karen tossed her head slightly. Her thick golden hair billowed in the breeze and fell gently against her shoulders. Better to answer him, she thought, and not get him needlessly riled.

Reluctantly she answered, "My name is Karen Barks. I was going with my . . . my father. Going with him to a college reunion at a place not far from here."

The giant raised one massive eyebrow and gave Karen a puzzled look. He then brought one enormous hand to his chin.

"Hmphf. Dr. Reid didn't know Barks was bringing any daughter along."

"Dr. Reid?" she inquired with surprise. "Then that must mean . . . that uniform you're wearing . . ."

He nodded affirmatively. "Yeah. I'm Grollman, his butler. And I know about this fraternity business. Fact is, that's why I was out in this neck of the woods. Dr. Reid told me to drive into town for some more booze. One of the guests already drunk up most of it. I was driving back to the house when I saw your headlights."

Karen automatically looked toward the car. The lights were gradually dimming, sapping off the battery's electric power, sending out beams that diffused amid the rolling fog. The insect gore that encrusted the roof, windows and sides of the vehicle were like some new coat of paint of hideous and indescribable colors. Karen shrugged, shuddering from the cold that swept through her.

Grollman's gaze followed Karen's to the car but he did not react, as though such sights were mundane.

"So you're here," said the giant butler. "But where's your father? After all, he was the one that got the invitation to this here party. Not you."

Again she began to cry. Her head turned slowly, almost mechanically, in the direction of the river. But then her head snapped back, eyes shut tightly, so as not to see the thing that had been her father. Tears welled in her eyes.

Noticing Karen's reaction to the river, Grollman looked in that direction. The moonlight illuminated the figure that lay with legs upon the bank and face submerged in the water. Even from such a distance great scarlet clots could be seen, contrasting with the whiteness of exposed bone.

Grollman trudged upon soggy ground to the river where he paused to look at the corpse. When he returned to Karen, the expression on his face had not changed.

"I'm sorry," he said. "But what's done is done. Now what are you gonna do? You can't stay out here. And you'd better shut off your headlights before the battery dies. Then you'll have to have your car towed outa here."

"I don't care what happens to the car. I never want to see it again."

"It's your crate, lady," he said coldly and raised one bushy eyebrow. "I can drive you to Dr. Reid's place. The group that's there ain't exactly your type. But you can't stay out here. That's for sure."

"Is there a phone there that I can use?"

"Sure. We ain't that far in the sticks."

Grollman made Karen uneasy, not only because of his brutish appearance, but because of his steady stare—like someone sizing up a side of beef. In the past she had been reluctant to hitchhike even on a main street during the brightest afternoon. But now she was considering a ride from this seven-foot-tall goon. Still, there was a phone.

"All right," she finally said. "Take me to Dr. Reid's and away from this awful place."

"This way," said Grollman. He resumed his giant steps that left deep shoeprints in the mudlike ground. "Careful where you step. The slime of this place can fool you. Sometimes it covers quicksand and there's plenty of quicksand in this swamp. Lucky I know this place like the back of my hand. I could probably hike it blindfolded."

Karen followed the giant butler, her hair streaming against

her face. The smell of lilies and orchids, the fleeting glimpses of bunchberries growing from the peat, would have thrilled her senses at any other time. But now they were part of the bog and the bog stood only for horror and death.

A black Cadillac limousine was parked halfway off the road. The wheels that rested upon the ground were one quarter buried in the soft surface of the bog. Karen knew little about cars. But she'd been photographed with Cadillacs and estimated this one to be about ten years old. The limousine was silhouetted against the moon like some dark behemoth, waiting silently. As Karen neared the Cadillac she saw that it probably hadn't been washed or polished in months, more likely years. The hubcaps were dull and dented. In all, this was a fitting vehicle for this shabby creature who called himself a butler.

Grollman opened the car door, then grasped Karen's hand with a strength that was startling. He could have crushed her had he so chosen. His fingers were not merely strong, they were also clammy. Karen yanked her hand from his grip and looked sternly into his face.

"I can get in myself, thank you."

Gracefully, with all the poise she had been taught and which was now like a reflex action, she slid onto the seat and over the ripped upholstery. Then she slammed the door shut.

Grollman entered the car from the other side and looked at his passenger. Again his eyes dwelled upon her, following the curves of her legs.

Self-consciously she made a futile effort to pull down the short dress.

His grin widened as he saw her struggle with the material. Then he started the engine of the Cadillac.

The hearselike limousine roared loudly as it prowled along the road that bordered on the left the great bog. The car passed the spot where Howard Barks' corpse still lay. As the car sped away, two orbs glowed faintly through the darkness.

Karen glimpsed the lights of the Fairlane as they finally dimmed and vanished in the darkness of the swamp.

The Cadillac finally stopped where the road ended to merge with the thickest area of the bog. Here birches, tamarack and swamp maple trees grew in their greatest profusion, creating a jungle of vegetation that reached skyward as if to blanket out the glowing moon. However, the foliage of the bog could not conceal the five other automobiles parked in the clearing where the road ended . . . or the mammoth structure that loomed awesome in the pale light.

Karen peered out the limousine window.

The house appeared to be a relic of some previous era of decadence and once might have been inhabited by some Civil War degenerates who killed and cannibalized wandering drunks in gray or blue uniforms. She wondered how the apparently rotting walls of the colonial mansion could even be standing. It should have been sucked into the bog ages ago.

Opulent once in previous decades, previous centuries, it now seemed fit only for throwing gnarled shadows and augmenting the morbid atmosphere of the swamp. There were lights beaming yellow behind the windows and black smoke twisted from the chimney to further obscure the moon.

She followed Grollman from the car. They walked along a pathway that was merely a place where plants did not grow. She could see the cracked, chipped wooden pillars that strained to support the warped eaves. Whatever color the building once had been was lost to forgotten memories. Wind blew through the trees, making them sway, causing them to creak. Was the mansion also swaying or was it her imagination, influenced by wavering shadows and her own fright?

They stepped carefully over the wooden porch, which miraculously, did not collapse.

Grollman began to reach for the rusted iron knob of the oaken door. But even as he reached for the doorknob, in a movement incredibly swift for a man who must have been in his middle fifties, snarling he captured a fly which had been buzzing around his hand.

"I hate bugs," he said, gritting his teeth. "But I hate flies most of all. Filthy little bastards, the way they hang around garbage and animal shit. And these kinda flies that come around at night are the worst of all. They'll bite you. Even drink your blood like vampire bugs. Filthy little bastards!"

With that, he slammed his palm against one of the wooden pillars, shaking it slightly and squashing the fly into an unrecognizable smear. The butler looked at his hand, then wiped it in the faded fabric of his trouser leg.

"Filthy little bastards," he complained a third time. Then he opened the door and held it until Karen entered.

"We're home."

The musty atmosphere assaulted Karen as the butler led her through the vestibule, down a gloomy hallway and then into the living room on the left. She rubbed her bare arms to stimulate some warmth. This was the coldest living room she had been in since the first days of the energy crisis. The furnishings could only be labeled as "early Charles Addams" for they matched no artistic scheme outside of a set from a horror film.

She coughed from the dust-filled air. Somehow dust had become a part of the interior design of the place. It covered virtually everything, every article of antique—no, junk—furniture. Grollman must have been as good a housekeeper as he was a butler. In fact, he seemed to have his own coating of dust.

He walked across the living room and stood before the far door. Then he motioned for Karen to join him. When he opened the door which led to the study, Karen gasped.

She had not expected to be confronted by anyone so suddenly, especially someone seated in a wheelchair, rolling forward and staring up at her through a pair of thick lensed dark glasses.

"And whom do we have here?" asked the man in the wheelchair slowly, his voice deeply pleasant.

His smooth, pale-complected face reflected hardly any emotion behind its concealment of dark glasses and a thick blond mustache and beard. His blond hair was combed straight back, meticulously. Although seated, with a khaki-colored woolen blanket draped across his motionless legs, he gave the feeling of being a tall man.

Grollman approached him and reported, "This is Karen Barks, Dr. Reid. Howard Barks' daughter."

"Oh," said Dr. Reid with pleasant surprise in his baritone voice but without changing his facial expression, "I didn't know Howard had a daughter. It's an honor, Karen. But where is your father? Shouldn't he be with you? Everyone else has been here for almost an hour."

Karen wanted to answer but was still overwhelmed by all the events of that night, including the sudden appearance of the man in the wheelchair.

"Bad news," Grollman finally broke in. "Her father's dead. It happened back there down the road. In the bog."

The butler's callous abruptness was distressing. Now Karen disliked the giant more than ever. His words sparked a flash of memory, the image of her father, the insects— She fought to suppress the tears she felt returning to her eyes.

"Oh, God, no!" said Dr. Reid, his voice revealing more warmth than his face. He took Karen's hand and clasped it. His dry warmth was assuring. "Karen—I hope you don't mind my calling you by your first name—I knew your father very well, over twenty-five years ago as a friend. Please accept my sympathy, Karen, because I can experience at least some of the grief you must be going through."

Karen sniffled as she dried her eyes.

Dr. Reid pushed his wheelchair forward and stopped only a few inches from her.

"That's better, Karen," he said. "Crying for the dead only hurts the living. If I may ask, how did it happen?"

It was Grollman who interjected, "The bog got him, doctor. Something in the bog. I saw the body myself."

"Grollman, do you always have to be so crude?"

Turning to the girl, he said, "Let me apologize for my butler, and if I can be of any help to you, don't hesitate to ask."

"I'd just like to use your telephone," she said.

"Certainly. Just follow me."

Dr. Reid swiveled his wheelchair about so that he faced the doorway through which he had come. Grollman held open the door while Dr. Reid and Karen entered the study.

She continued to observe the furnishings. More junk and more dust, if that were possible. The study was equal to or worse than the living room. Yet, there were new furnishings in this room that gave it a weird prominence over the room she had just left. The walls seemed built of books, so numerous that their leather covers almost blended together. She saw more of the large and, strangely enough, highly polished mahogany table that occupied the center of the room. A group of men sat about the table, but she saw them only fleetingly as she followed Dr. Reid to the telephone. It was an old model, one she hadn't realized was still in use anywhere and was mounted on the wall between two filled bookcases.

As Karen placed the receiver to her ear and dialed the operator, she could hear Dr. Reid telling the small group what had befallen her father and heard their collective shocked sigh of surprise.

"Highway Patrol, please," she said into the mouthpiece.

She turned, waiting for the operator to make the connection, and saw the men sitting around the table. Some of them were vested with such peculiarities that they seemed as much at home in this old house as Grollman. God! she thought. Were these the men with whom her father had once so closely assoicated?

CHAPTER THREE

The unmarked Highway Patrol sedan sped along the straight stretch of road that formed the border of the swampland. The smells of the bog, the vapors that issued from dead animals and decomposing vegetation wafted through the open windows. The two plainclothes officers riding in the car showed clearly their aversion to the odor.

Sgt. Gary Rutledge was almost grateful for the sounds of the insects, the chipping and creaking of unseen yet present life that existed somewhere in the shadows of the bog. They interrupted the monotonous purr of the car's engine, and anything that broke the detective's boredom on a dismal night like this could elicit his gratitude.

"You'll be glad when tonight's over, won't you?" said the man seated next to him. Vincent Cordoni, Gary's partner, a mature-looking sergeant of twenty-seven, was only one year younger than he. He smiled as if he knew what was foremost in Gary's mind.

"Damn right," said Gary exhaling a big gust of air from his

lungs. "My vacation officially starts on Monday. But believe me, I'm going to start living it bright and early tomorrow noon—when I get out of bed. Ah, I can see it now. Three weeks of doing nothing except taking it easy. No more driving out to some God forsaken place like this bog on what'll probably will turn out to be nothing but another crank call."

The police car skirred along the road until the road was devoured by the thickness of the swamp. The vehicle stopped in a semi-clearing where six other vehicles—one of which was an old Cadillac limousine—were parked among the swamp maple and birch trees.

"This looks like the place, Vince," said Gary drolly. "No need to look at the address; there isn't another house around here anywhere."

"I wonder who lives here," remarked Vincent Cordoni. "If I didn't know that Bela Lugosi has been dead for years, I'd swear this was his summer cottage."

The mansion was like some ancient tomb, so out of place looming above such modern machines as automobiles. Yet, there was a dark majesty about the place. Gary was a bit awe struck as he got out of the car and, accompanied by his partner, stepped into the marsion's expansive shadow.

"It's a weird place, all right," said Gary. "But this is where that Barks girl called from."

Gary straightened his tie, then adjusted the shoulders of his inexpensive, dark gray sports coat. Briskly, he stepped across the porch and knocked on the oak door.

The door opened. The tall butler looked down upon the detectives' six-foot heights. Then, wrinkling the skin of his forehead, the giant spoke.

"You're the ones from the highway patrol?"

Vincent flashed his badge. "Yes. A Karen Barks phoned headquarters and gave this address. Is she here?"

"She's here, all right," said the butler. "My name is Groll-man, I work here. She's waiting inside."

The detectives had been trained to observe so they scrutinized as much of the dirty furnishings as their fast pace permitted. Walking down a long corridor, they stopped before a closed door—the second door on the left in that dimly lit hallway.

Gary removed a pack of Camels from his shirt pocket and tapped out a cigarette. He lit the cigarette with his disposable butane lighter, sucking in the strong smoke and coughing slightly. He didn't really enjoy smoking and the way it made his lungs burn. But on occasions like this, when his mind began to flash on corpses—or the possibility of there being corpses—he splurged. He spit a few shreds of unfiltered tobacco onto the worn brownish rug, then, followed by Vincent, pursued the butler into the study.

Gary's eyes registered fast, moving rapidly about the room. He was accustomed to perceive scenes as a whole as if his eyes had snapped a photograph which he could study later. There were books seemingly everywhere in the study. Books with titles in gold stamping, the ones nearer to him boasting such names as *Ecology—Addresses, Essays and Lectures, The Co-lumbian Exchange; Biological and Cultural Consequences of 1492; The Arena of Life: The Dynamics of Ecology* and *The Closing Circle; Nature, Man and Technology.* He observed books with more general titles such as *Ecology, Conservation* and *Environmental Control.* There were also some black and white posters on the wall that—

But he quickly shifted his attention to the people in the study. There were six men seated around the table. And there was a young woman. She sat in an old arm chair from which the stuffings showed in several places. The redness of her eyes betrayed the fact that she had been crying only recently. Gary also saw that she was extremely beautiful, with a body that was the closest to perfection he had ever seen. She was also startlingly familiar.

"Are you the lady who called?"

"Yes," she replied in a strangled voice.

"My father," she began, softly and with effort, "and I were driving here through the bog, when . . . when . . ."

She choked as she spoke but finally managed to blurt out the story that made even the two highway patrol sergeants exchange looks of disbelief. The other men in the room sitting about the dining table began to squirm nervously and murmur amongst themselves. Their eyes were large, some of their faces pale.

"Now, Miss, I realize you're upset, but that's a pretty weird tale. I'm not saying I don't believe you, mind you. But I've never heard a story like yours in all my seven years on the force."

"I don't care what you've never heard, sergeant," she cried. "But that's the way it happened." She began to cry. "Honest to God, that's what happened."

Gary had heard enough people lie. But this young woman seemed to believe her bizarre story. Either that or else she was some fine actress with a not-too-convincing script. If such a corpse existed, there might be a killer—not in the form of beetles but human beings.

"OK, honey, we'll go take a look. But first I want a quick run down on who all you guys are, and what you're doing here," Rutledge said.

"From the looks of all those glasses I'd say you've got some sort of a party going on." Added Cordoni. "You can begin," he nodded to the man in the wheelchair.

"Dr. Ronald Reid. This is my house."

"Medical doctor?" queried Sgt. Rutledge.

"No, Sgt. Rutledge. I have a Ph.D. in chemistry. But being confined to a wheelchair doesn't give me much opportunity to put that degree to use.'' Self-consciously Dr. Reid lowered his head and looked down at the khaki blanket that concealed his legs.

He moved his wheelchair between the two detectives. Indicating the group at the table, he continued.

''Howard Barks, Karen's father, and we seven used to belong to the same fraternity back in college,'' he said. ''We hadn't seen each other in twenty-five years. This was to have been our first reunion.''

''Seems like a hell of a way to start a reunion party,'' growled Gary. ''Major, you're next.''

The obese man seated nearest to Gary was drumming his fingers against the smooth tabletop. He wore an old yet well-kept Army uniform, but one which had obviously seen better years. The major's gold insignias on his shoulders and the medals worn over his heart were gleaming, probably polished earlier that day. But the major had apparently accumulated so much bulk since the uniform was issued that the material seemed more to encase than cover him.

''My name is Alex Gear,'' the man said in pompous voice as though he were announcing himself to a commanding officer. ''*Major* Alex Gear, retired.''

''World War II?'' asked Gary.

''Korea'' returned the Major, sniffing so that his impeccably groomed white handlebar mustache wriggled.

''And you?'' asked Gary to the rather ordinary man seated next to him. Ordinary except for a pair of glasses which seemed to be made from the bottoms of coke bottles and except for a peculiar twitching of the right cheek which became more agitated when the detective spoke to him.

Self-consciously the man adjusted his thick-lensed glasses and took a few puffs on his pipe, the bowl of which was carved into the miniature head of a sabre-toothed cat. The smoke settled about the table as a sweet smelling cloud.

"I am Dr. William Bertrand," he said in a throaty, almost hoarse, voice. "I am a scientist, sergeant. A paleontologist for the Marshall Natural History Museum. I study prehistoric life forms—fossil invertebrates in particular."

"And you sir?"

The next man seemed quite opposite to the others in appearance. He had a week old growth of beard on his pitiful face. His faded navy blue suit cut in the double-breasted style of the Forties was a Salvation Army original, and fit poorly, thought Gary. His eyes were glassy and as he raised his almost empty glass, tried to keep it from shaking, then downed the remainder of the golden-brown liquid. His bloodshot eyes looked at Gary with a newborn confidence.

"Hello, sergeant," he slurred. "*I* am Bryant Krass. And unlike these other illustrious gents, I don't do a hell of a lot of anything! Least, not anymore. But there's one thing I can still do better than anyone else in this place."

Laughing, Krass reached across the table for the half-empty bottle of Bacardi Puerto Rican rum and refilled his glass almost to the top.

Gary turned to the man sitting at the head of the table.

"You?"

Of the entire group, he was the least conspicuous. He wore a conventional and contemporary business suit. Probably cost over a hundred dollars, the detective thought. The man's graying hair was neatly cut. And there was a look of anxiety upon his rather average looking face. Furtively his eyes darted about, looking at each of the other members of the fraternity, and then at Gary.

"Kessler," he said in a quick blast of sound. "Richard Kessler. Sales representative with the Greenberg Insurance Company."

"Fine," answered Gary.

The man on Kessler's left almost made Gary Rutledge laugh. He could see that Vincent was also restraining himself. Wearing a suit of garrish red, green and yellow plaid, and with an obvious black toupee, he seemed to have sprung from the latest and weirdest men's fashion magazine. *Flaming Whackos Illustrated,* Gary thought with a faint chuckle escaping his throat.

Smiling so that the wrinkles in his apparently powdered face took on the semblance of a relief map of someplace Gary wouldn't like to visit, the man replied in a husky voice, "My name is Lance. Harvey Lance."

"And what do you do, Mr., er, Lance?" asked Gary.

"I am a collector, sergeant. A collector of *Lepidoptera*.

"No, I mean what do you do for a living? Surely not collect butterflies."

"Of course not. Collecting *Lepidoptera* is just a hobby. But actually I don't do anything for a living. I don't need to."

The last man at the table, seated close to Gary's right, was a small ineffectual looking gentleman, almost totally bald and with a small surgical scar extending upward from the end of his left eyebrow.

"You?" asked Paul.

"Samuel Tate, officer," said the man as a proud look suddenly swept across his somewhat homely face. "And as a matter of fact, I used to be in the same business as you."

"Do tell."

"I was a private investigator for a large detective agency for twenty years. But my heart went bad. So I've taken to writing mystery novels. Maybe you've read some of them?"

"Sorry, I've never read any of them, Mr. Tate."

Vincent winked from across the room.

"I'll sum things up as briefly as I can," Gary addressed them all. "Miss Barks telephoned highway patrol headquarters and said that her father had been killed. Now she tells me that he was killed by insects. Obviously I haven't yet seen the body."

"I've seen it," said Grollman. "And believe me, it ain't a pretty sight."

"I haven't seen it," Gary went on, "but I do find it hard to believe that a swarm of insects would first attack a moving car, and then single out the driver and let the passenger off without a scrape."

"You sound like you think maybe one of us might have done this," said Bryant Krass with a sly wet grin on his greasy face and an empty glass in his greasy hand.

"I'm not saying anyone did anything—yet. Remember, so far I haven't seen a body. But we're going out there now. And then I'm going to need some answers, perhaps from all of you."

The men at the table exchanged looks of consternation.

"Perhaps two of us can be of some help, Sergeant."

It was the one who had identified himself as Dr. William Bertrand.

"How do you mean?" asked Gary.

"I am a paleontologist," began Dr. Betrand. "But—

"We're not interested in prehistoric insects right now," interrupted Rutledge impatiently.

"I know, Sergeant. But just because my field is invertebrate paleo, that doesn't mean I don't know a great deal about today's insects."

"What are you getting at, Doctor?"

"I mean, if you're willing to forget for a while that I might be a murderer and accept my scientific opinions, I might be able to ascertain merely by examining the corpse, whether insects could really have done this terrible thing."

"Sounds reasonable. But you said something about two of you being able to help. Are you talking about Mr. Harvey here?"

"That's Mr. Lance," the man in the red-green-and-yellow suit interrupted. "No, I wouldn't be of much help. All I know about is *Lepidoptera*. And surely no amount of butterflies could ever cause a man's death."

"I think Willie means me," came a voice to Gary's right.

"You, Dr. Reid? But I thought your field was chemistry."

"It is. But I do have some knowledge of entomology. When I was a boy I had made a hobby out of insects."

"Hmmm," said Gary. "So it looks like there are three men here who know something about insects. All right, then, I'll radio headquarters from the car. Then the five of us will take a little trip into the bog."

"The five of us?" asked Dr. Bertrand.

"You, Dr. Reid, Sgt. Cordoni, me and Miss Barks."

"No," she protested, "please don't ask me to go back there. Grollman can show you the way. But please let me stay here. I couldn't stand going back there after what I saw."

She walked to the heavily draped study window, and Gary could hear her muffled sobs.

"Listen, Miss Barks. I'm sorry if I've sounded like a machine all night. I won't ask you to come along. Only please try to understand that I'm trying to do my job."

Gary smiled at her encouragingly and saw that she was attempting to return the smile. Then he looked about the room and made a slight gesture, something of a salute, to Vincent Cordoni.

"All right, then," said Gary commandingly, "the four of us are going into the bog. Meanwhile, you're all to wait here until we get back."

CHAPTER FOUR

Sgt. Gary Rutledge had seen corpses before in his job but never one quite like this. Never one this bad, he thought—this disgusting.

Repulsive! he groaned to himself. Even more repulsive than what that axe killer had done last summer to the old widow recluse—what was her name again?—the widow who lived in that shack in the hills. Gary had not seen her hacked up remains except in police photographs. No, he somehow never managed to draw an assignment that was material for newspaper headlines. Why did he always have to get the cases that no one except the tabloids really gave a damn about? Like the case in which that poor slob was accidentally run down by a Mack truck. Or the time that drunken hunter stumbled over his own shotgun and blew off most of his stupid head. Or cases like this one, repulsive but if the death were caused by insects, hardly worthy of the front page of the *Times*.

Gary was smoking his second cigarette since he had driven to Dr. Reid's mansion in response to Karen Barks' call. The smoke was strong, distasteful. It wafted in the warm breeze and drifted over the green scummed river in which the corpse of Howard Barks floated.

The abandoned Ford Fairlane also seemed to be a corpse. The light of its facsimile eyes had died. And its metal skin was coated with an unsightly crusty mass that suggested decomposition.

The full moon was not the only source of illumination in the bog. The darkness and the fog were brightly pierced by the beams of five vehicles. One vehicle was Gary's official sedan, with its headlights and spotlight trained toward the river. There were also lights shining from two big Harley-Davidson motorcycles with highway patrol markings, from Dr. Reid's Cadillac limousine and from an ambulance, the latter also adorned with a revolving red and white light. All five vehicles were parked halfway off the road.

The two uniformed highway patrol officers stood near the dark and abandoned Fairlane. One of them rested his hand atop the butt of his regulation .38 revolver as though he anticipated the appearance of some hungry alligator slithering from the dense foliage.

The pair of white-outfitted ambulance attendants opened the door at the rear of their vehicle. Then they removed a stretcher from the ambulance and wheeled it across the cracked ground and toward the half-submerged corpse.

Standing in the pudding-like ground were Gary Rutledge, Vincent Cordoni and the paleontologist, Dr. William Bertrand. They looked again at the corpse and then toward the parked Cadillac. Within moments Grollman removed the collapsible wheelchair from the back seat and pulled it into shape. He lifted Dr. Reid from the front seat of the limousine and gently set him into the chair. The action was efficiently routine. Then Grollman pushed his employer's wheelchair toward the riverbank, producing tracks like miniature earthquake fissures in the moonlit moss.

Gary did not turn away as the ambulance attendants went into their routine. Instead he dragged hard on his Camel, and didn't even cough as he felt the internal warmth from the smoke which he hoped would compensate for the chills racing along his backbone. He pulled his sports coat tight against his muscular frame but the chill was still there.

The attendants yanked the corpse by its skeletal legs onto the soggy embankment, leaving a wake of gore behind. Casually they lifted the body, turned it over, and dropped it onto the stretcher, affording Gary and the two scientists a better look.

Better? Worse was more accurate. The black hollow sockets of the corpse stared sightlessly at the black sky. The mouth was hardly more than a black cavity, locked in some silent scream. There was little of the face left but enough remained for Drs. Bertrand and Reid to discern the external features they had once known.

"Well," Gary began, looking first at the paleontologist and then at the man in the wheelchair, "what's the verdict?"

First, Dr. Bertrand touched the substance that encrusted the Ford Fairlane. His right cheek began to flutter. Raising his left index finger, now covered with the same brownish muck, before his eyes, he puffed on his pipe and nodded affirmatively. "These are the remains of insects all right."

Gary could smell the sweetness of Bertrand's pipe, which then mingled with the odors of the night, as he looked to Dr. Reid for a response.

"There's really not much to look at," said Dr. Reid. "But there's enough of a face left to see that it could be Howard Barks. Of course, it's been twenty-seven years for me. We all change over the years but . . . Yes, I'd say that this could have been Howard Barks."

''There's a better way to make sure,'' said Vincent Cordoni.

''Right,'' answered Gary.

Gary's eyes shifted. They scanned the myriad forms of odd vegetation, then stopped at a sizable branch of birch wood. He grasped the branch estimating its weight at several pounds, then used it to turn the corpse over on its side. Feeling for the body's wallet, he removed it. A quick search through the wallet produced a soggy Selective Service card, a driver's license and two credit cards, all bearing the name of Howard Barks.

''This confirms the body's identity,'' said Gary dispassionately. ''It's Barks all right. But this still doesn't prove anything about insects attacking him. But at least we can forget any ideas that he was killed by somebody up at the mansion.''

''Yup!'' said Vincent. ''Seems to me like there isn't much need for an investigation. Unless you want to arrest an alligator or something.''

The officer, whose hand still rested on his gun butt, nodded. ''God only knows how many different kinds of man-eaters could be hiding in this wilderness.''

''Well?'' Gary asked Dr. Bertrand, then shot an inquisitive glance at Dr. Reid. ''Are you two willing to put your reputations on the line and give me an opinion?''

''That's why we're here,'' answered Dr. Bertrand. ''I'm willing to make an educated guess.''

''And even though I've mainly been thinking about chemistry, I'll also give it a try,'' added Dr. Reid.

The ambulance attendants waited expectantly until Vincent Cordoni gave them a nod. Then the two men in white grabbed opposite ends of a spotless white sheet with which they neatly covered the torn and bloodied remains of Howard Barks. A black and crimson stain oozed through the clean fabric, revealing the outline of the thing beneath.

Gary rubbed his callused fingers through his crop of thick

black hair, which he wore as long as department regulations permitted. "Thank God that's that," he said. "This has got to be the worst one I'll ever see."

He watched as the two attendants deposited the corpse into the rear end of the ambulance. He saw the two motorcycle officers sigh with relief as the attendants slammed the rear door of the ambulance, thereby forever hiding that monstrosity from everyone's sight.

One of the attendants called out, his voice carrying over the noises made by unseen life. "Will you be needing us for anything else, Sergeant? It's getting late and we'd like to take this body out to the hospital, get the doc to give him a quick D.O.A. and then drop him off at the morgue."

"Yeah, how about us?" asked the other motorcycle officer.

"You guys can all take off," said Gary. "Nothing more for you to do around here. Go home and get some sleep, if you *can* sleep after looking at this mess."

"You want me to radio in the report while you talk to the doctors?" asked Vincent Cordoni.

"Yeah, I'd appreciate that, Vince."

Relief was apparent on the two officers' faces as they revved up the engines of their motorcycles. Waving salutes, they roared away to become small dots of light in the distant blackness. Less than a minute later the ambulance, too, vanished down the road.

While Vincent called headquarters, Gary returned to the scientists.

"Well then," he began, "what conclusion have you two reached. Could the girl's story be true? Could Howard Barks have been attacked by a horde of beetles and eaten alive until he looked like . . . like that?"

"From what I know of insects," said Dr. William Bertrand, peering into the detective's eyes through the almost translucent eyeglass lenses, "and from what I've seen them do on a small scale, I would say that it is entirely possible that insects are responsible for Howard's death."

"My interest in insects never went beyond studying their habits and collecting them," said Dr. Reid, "but I won't doubt the possibility."

"What about the possibility of an animal?" asked Gary. "Like an alligator?"

"No," said Dr. Reid, "I don't believe it could have been anything like an alligator. There were no bones broken. If it had been an alligator Howard would have been torn apart by the reptile's jaws. Howard seemed to have been neatly stripped of his flesh. Almost flayed. Eaten."

"Hmmm. And I thought that Tate character was the ex-detective. But you two aren't doing bad yourselves."

Dr. Bertrand's face was encircled by a wreath of blue-gray pipe smoke. "Tell me, Sgt. Rutledge, have you ever read the story 'Leiningen Versus the Ants,' by Carl Stephenson?"

"Back in high school, I think. But I remember the movie version with Charlton Heston."

"Well, Sergeant," the paleontologist went on, "that story might sound rather far-fetched. But there actually are ants like that which can sweep across a territory, stripping the flesh off everything they can find to satisfy their appetites. In the tropics, the *Dorylinae*—or army ants—sometimes move across the land, eating small mammals and arthropods. But under certain and sometimes extraordinary conditions, those critters will strip clean the flesh of larger animals, including humans.

"Furthermore, Sergeant, I've examined the residue that covers so much of Howard's car and I'd stake my reputation that it is composed of thousands of dead insects."

"All right, I guess you've convinced me that bugs could have done this grisly thing. Let's assume, then, that thousands of insects smashed themselves against Barks' car. Then thousands more came and ate him alive. Okay. There's still one big question that needs answering. And that question is *Why?* What would cause thousands of brainless insects to single out this one car . . . then this one man . . . and eat him alive?"

Dr. Bertrand paused thoughtfully. He took several steps toward the river, then turned, glasses reflecting the moonlight, and looked back at the others. Stroking his narrow chin, he said, "Of course you've heard a great deal about ecology these days. It's become quite the fad. A shame, perhaps, since fads have a tendency to eventually become obsolete and ignored. But it is possible, Sergeant, that something has happened that could have changed the environment of this swamp—a change which may have resulted in an anomaly in the insects' behavior. The alteration of one ecological factor can change the normal habits of an entire population of insects."

"What kind of factor," asked Gary.

"I'll give you an example. Certain insects are parasites, feeding off other insects or on the bodies of animals. Now suppose these food insects or animals are exterminated, either by DDT or by toxic waste products dumped into a body of water, like this river. If the consumer insects are somehow deprived of their normal source of nourishment, they will then proceed to feed upon other life forms. Consider, Sergeant, that the insects outnumber every other life form on this planet—with over 625,000 varieties. Then consider what would happen if the food supplies of vast numbers of these millions upon millions of insects were destroyed.

"The deprived insects would change their diet. Remember that Nature is like some complicated chain. Break one link in that chain, such as the elimination of a population's food supply, and the entire chain becomes disrupted. Who knows what has been sprayed over this infested swampland or what has been dumped into that river over the years? But it is indeed possible that some link or links in the ecological chain have been broken here and that caused those critters to attack poor Howard.

"We must also remember that insects are more complex than most people suspect. Certain species of flies, for example, have developed resistances to the insecticides that Man has invented. The implications are staggering. For we develop chemicals for the purpose of killing off vast numbers of flies—chemicals which can also destroy plant life, pollute our waters and lands—and then the flies live and continue to procreate while our planet dies. In other words, insects could very well take over this world by merely significantly upsetting their ways of life. They outnumber us ridiculously. And they were on this Earth millions of years before the first man shed his tail. They could still be here, in greater number, when the last man dies of his own follies."

"That's all very interesting," said Gary, noticing that Vincent was getting out of the patrol car to rejoin the small group. "But you still haven't given me an explanation as to why the bugs attacked only Howard Barks and not his daughter."

Dr. Reid lifted his head as if to look about for any flying insects in his proximity, then replied, "Perhaps Karen wasn't part of that broken chain Willie was talking about. Nature is mysterious. And I don't presume to understand her strange ways."

"Or maybe the bugs just weren't hungry anymore, eh?" said Gary. Then he shuddered for he could hear the insect noises resounding through the bog, sounds which helped to conjure all manners of unpleasant thoughts in his imagination. There was a sudden flash image of Karen's lovely flesh being bitten away by bugs— "Come on," he interrupted his own daydream nightmare, "let's get the hell out of this place before I go buggy."

Minutes later, Gary Rutledge, his partner, and the other three men were back in Reid's mansion.

No one had left the house. The ex-fraternity members were milling about the study, apparently occupied with other matters than thoughts of Howard Barks. Richard Kessler sat nervously at the table, wringing his hands together as the group returning from the bog entered the study. Samuel Tate was now seated in the poorly upholstered armchair. Harvey Lance browsed through a textbook on butterflies which he had somehow discovered amongst the books. Pacing about was the overweight major, who suddenly snapped to a semblance of attention as the detectives walked across the room. Bryant Krass was the only other man still seated at the refectory table, and he was occupied with a half empty V.O. Canadian whiskey.

Karen Barks turned away from the window and looked searchingly into Gary's eyes.

The major was the first to speak. "Well? What do you have to report, Sergeant Rutledge?"

"You can all go home," he announced, "unless you'd rather keep celebrating your reunion in light of what's happened tonight. We found Howard Barks."

"Then—" started Karen.

Gary looked at her sadly. He saw the look of grim expectancy on her beautiful face, saw the way her brown eyes seemed to beg for an answer.

"Apparently it was as you said, Miss Barks," answered Gary. "I'm sorry for not believing you back then. But it's my job to investigate and not just believe."

Harvey Lance replaced his butterfly book on the shelf, letting it vanish amongst the plethora of leather book spines. He turned, and, with a theatrical gesture of his hand addressed the other members of the old fraternity. "Then there is no use in our staying any longer in this gloomy place.''

''I agree,'' said Tate. ''Things have gotten a little too morbid around here for me, even though for a while I thought we'd have a real mystery on our hands.''

''I suggest,'' said Kessler looking about furtively, ''that we temporarily postpone our reunion and get together later this week when things aren't so tense. And at the risk of offending Ronald, I think we should meet somewhere else, someplace not so far out of the way or associated with bad memories.''

''Someplace like Kelly's,'' said Bryant Krass with a wet leer. ''Like in the old days.''

The other members of the fraternity mumbled in agreement.

''And what about you Miss Barks?'' asked Vincent. ''What are you going to do?''

''Go home, I suppose,'' she said.

''But your car—'' Gary began, again smelling her intoxicating perfume and watching the way her long hair seemed to glow in the dim light of the study.

''Leave it there. Have it towed away. I don't care. I never want to see it again. But I'll make it home okay. A taxi—''

''Can I take you home in the patrol car?''

She nodded and managed a small smile though the sadness had not left her eyes. She moved closer to him, enough for him to determine her perfume was jasmine. Instantly jasmine became Gary's favorite scent.

Gary led her through the mildewed mansion and out the door. They stopped on the porch. From behind them they heard snatches of conversation.

''Will you join us at Kelly's, Ronald?''

''I'm sorry, but I'd better refuse, Sam. This wheelchair doesn't let me go out very often. That's why I wanted to have the reunion here.''

"Then you won't be angry if we continue this reunion some other time and at Kelly's?"

"Of course not. You fellows managed to survive without me after I quit school. You'll continue, I'm sure."

Gary led Karen from the squeaking porch steps and toward the parked squad car. Cordoni was already riding shotgun in the front seat. Turning back to the mansion, Gary could see that Dr. Reid and his guests were still conversing. Standing at the side of the building, half obscured by the shadow thrown by a large swamp maple towering against the moon, was the butler Grollman. He seemed to be watching the group. Or listening.

There was another who watched—one who had sensed the summoning of the Call.

That one was Grillus.

From the darkness of his dank burrow, Grillus responded. Anxiously he gripped the moist walls of his home with the spikes that adorned his hind legs. When he emerged from the pit the moss beneath him was like a soft carpet of moon-kissed green. The moss contrasted colorfully against the yellow markings on his back, markings resembling miniature fans.

Other crickets were scrambling about, moving to acknowledge Grillus as their leader. Yet Grillus sensed that he was not their overlord. He could never truly command the others as long as forces over which he had no control existed.

Grillus rubbed his back legs across the sides of his abdomen, proudly producing the sound so characteristic of his kind.

The others responded, moving their own legs in identical fashion. Their tympana membranes vibrated, creating a symphony of mutual stridulations. Hundreds of crickets were assembling before Grillus. They increased the vehemence with which they produced their rhythmic chirrups.

Yet something was wrong. Grillus knew.

This was not the mating season. These were not tunes for serenading females. Why else should Grillus conduct his choir with such exhuberance?

Grillus lifted his black head, his twin antennae waved in the cool breeze. He perceived blurry shapes looming in the distance, shapes which moved from the great angular mountain like titanic monsters of the fog. These were the shapes of gods or demons, shapes that Grillus knew were the designated ones.

The crickets often warned against an approaching enemy. But these lumbering forms were not the predators, and so there should be no cause to stridulate. For those were the motives to chirrup—mating and warning—relayed instinctively from one to another.

There could be only one other reason why Grillus and his followers should carry on in such fashion.

The shapes now stood before larger shapes. Shapes sleek and rounded, several of which reflected the moonlight like the black-green surface of the river. Would the hunger come again? The hunger that Grillus had felt before when he and his followers were somehow guided to attack that unknown four-legged animal? Would hate return? Or, perhaps, the urge to mate?

But Grillus knew that these ponderous shapes constituted the enemy. Though, if not by hunger or hatred, why were he and his brothers summoned from their burrows to crawl upon the soft moss? Grillus did not know and could only obey.

Another walked among them. One whose prominence even superceded that of Grillus. The newcomer was larger than Grillus or any of his brethren. He was, in fact, a most formidable creature. Had it not been for that external force, the crickets would have been chirruping in warning against the approach of this portentious monster. Now, however, the crickets waited like some great army anticipating the commands of a far greater general.

Grillus moved before the newcomer, halting and lowering his head to acknowledge his supremacy. And of the newcomer's supremacy there was no doubt. He stood in a strange position, front legs tucked beneath his face, but for Mantis the position was perfectly natural, to await his prey.

An answer. That was what Grillus demanded.

Grillus and Mantis confronted one another. They had no rapport according to the Way. Mantis should have, without the slightest hesitation, satisfied his voracious appetite with the cricket's smaller body. But that was according to the Way, and on this night the Call reigned supreme.

Mantis turned from Grillus, his large eyes attempting to focus on the darkly moving shapes.

Antennae moved atop Mantis' demon head and then touched those of Grillus.

There was no longer confusion in Grillus' brain.

No, the praying mantis had told him, this was not the time to attack. This was not the moment to feast upon forbidden food. Now was the time merely to observe and remember these tremendous shapes, perhaps until the hunger returned.

Mantis and Grillus and the innumerable army of crickets watched as the shapes entered their sleeping dragons, awakened their burning eyes, and then vanished into the void at the end of the world.

CHAPTER FIVE

In the old days everyone went to Kelly's. Those were great times! Kelly's Pub had not changed much since Bryant Krass and the other members of the fraternity attended college. The small tavern was literally across the street from the campus. But Kelly's was almost accepted as part of college property. The place offered students a kind of last class of the day. Almost everyone stopped by Kelly's before returning home to cram for the next day's quiz or finally getting down to some serious plagiarism for the term paper due the following week.

Four nights after the death of Howard Barks, a rather extraordinarily clear night at that, the atmosphere at Kelly's was the same smelly cloud it had always been. The air was thick with the stink of beer and smoke.

Bryant Krass and the other five men gathered at a rectangular table in the farthest corner of the pub could swear that this was the same cloud of smoke that had selected Kelly's as its home even before they had attended the university. The fact that the smoke irritated the eyes and lungs didn't matter. Krass and his friends had endured the unpleasant smoke a quarter century ago and they'd do it again tonight.

They also endured the noise. No one seemed to care that his voice was often inaudible over the cacophony of glass beer mugs clunking against each other and thumping atop the wooden tables, or above the singing, laughing, shouting of the generally younger clientele from the college. Or the relentless blaring of last season's music from the old juke box in the center of the room.

Why should the six men mind? This was Kelly's just as it had always been, just as it had been so fondly stored in their nostalgic memories. Kelly's—one spot in the ever crowding ever changing world that was virtually unmarred by time. This was the Kelly's they had loved in their fraternity days. Now they realized that old loves can be reborn.

"Ah, Kelly's," said Bryant Krass, lifting a full mug of beer to his moist lips and gulping down the bitter contents in one long swallow. He lowered the empty glass from his foamy lips and slammed it hard against the table near the "B.K." that he had carved into the wood over twenty-five years ago. Wiping his mouth, he continued, "But the days when I used to come here for beer have gone. I rarely drink beer anymore." He turned his head to the left and looked at the bar. "Hey," he said loud enough to be heard above a scratchy rock recording, "bring me something with a little more pazazz, bartender! Whiskey! A bottle!"

The bartender motioned to a youthful bus boy who brought the unopened bottle and a shot glass over to the table.

Anxiously Krass opened the bottle, filled the whiskey glass and downed the bronze-colored liquid in almost one motion. The alcohol hardly burned his throat for he had become proficient at drinking some years ago and now it was almost like breathing.

He looked at the other men crowded about the small table. Next to him on the left was Maj. Alex Gear, in tight-fitting uniform. To Gear's left, Harvey Lance played with delicate fingers against the smoothness of his half filled mug. Dr. William Bertrand, seated to Krass' right, contributed to the smoky atmosphere with his sabre-tooth pipe and poured himself a full mug of beer from the glass pitcher resting in the center of the table. And to the paleontologist's right, Samuel Tate and Richard Kessler took slow sips from their own almost-full glasses of beer.

"Yes, Kelly's," Dr. William Bertrand reminisced, lifting his glass. His thick glasses almost touched the foam as he took a lingering drink. "I can remember when I'd come in here right after zoology class, sit down at this same table and in this same seat, I think. I used to be able to chug-a-lug almost a whole pitcher back then."

"That was a long time ago, Willie," said Richard Kessler. His fingers were nervously patting his glass. For several moments he stared into smoke-filled space, thinking. "That was before you began devoting most of your time to old bones instead of beer—and before I started selling insurance."

"I know," said Harvey Lance. There was a slight look of disdain on his lined face. His smooth fingers pressed into place several hairs of his black toupee. "Bones of a Brontosaurus or something?"

"If you're talking about the critter I helped to prepare at the museum a few years back, you mean *Apatosaurus excelsus*, commonly and incorrectly referred to by the public as Brontosaurus. But I've got to admit that going to Hall 38 at the museum where the fossil vertebrates are on display and looking at that brute does give me more satisfaction than being able to chug-a-lug a full pitcher of beer. Anyway, I only did a little work on that critter. Remember I'm in invertebrate paleo. It's less strenuous work for an aging dinosaur like myself."

Samuel Tate leaned forward on the tabletop. His eyes shifted, looking individually at the five men. The large pitcher of beer almost hid his small frame. "I guess we've all changed in the past twenty-five years. We all look a little different, especially me, I guess. Used to be heavier when we met here and when I had great aspirations to being a great private eye. And now it's Dick with his insurance policies, Willie with his fossils, Alex with his army nostalgia—"

"Yeah," interrupted Krass, then finishing off the contents of another glass of whiskey. "And poor Bryant hasn't changed a bit ever since he flunked out of his senior year and found that a bottle gave more security than another year or two of classes. No, I haven't changed a damn bit. But neither has old Harv. Good ol' Harv is as fruity as ever."

"Now just a minute!" said Harvey Lance. He started to rise from his chair when the Major grabbed his arm and forced him back down.

"Here now, Harvey," said Alex Gear, "let's not get disorderly. This is supposed to be a reunion and not the resuming of an old battle."

"But Bryant can't talk to me like that. This isn't twenty-five years ago, you know."

"Don't let it get to you," said Kessler from across the table. "Bryant's just kidding. He was always a kidder. And he's had too much to drink."

"If you ask me," said Lance, "Bryant's been having too much to drink since he flunked out of school."

"Nobody did ask you," said Krass with an unsightly grin. "Sorry if I offended you, Harv ol' pal. I guess if you want to go about with your little net catching butterflies that's your business. That is, till some other guys in white start looking for you with their nets.''

Krass let his eyes bore into Lance's so that the man in the dark hairpiece and yellow and brown suit squirmed in his seat. The image of the butterfly collector was not as sharp as it had been earlier that night. The whiskey in Krass' stomach was already warming him like a furnace. To complete his indignity upon Harvey Lance, he raised and lowered his eyebrows three times.

Then Krass turned to Dr. Bertrand.

''Looks like I'm the only one who can still chug-a-lug with the best of them,'' said Krass. ''So you can see that at least one of us hasn't been shot all to hell.''

Until now the group had been avoiding any mention of Howard Barks and the unfortunate incident in the bog. But Bryant Krass' blood was racing, shooting new confidence and audacity through his body. He smiled, then poured and quaffed another full glass of whiskey. The taste was almost nonexistent now but the effects were more noticeable than ever.

''Really too bad about Howard,'' he said. The name of the dead fraternity brother was followed by a loud hiccup. ''Getting eaten by bugs like that. And I always liked that guy.''

The men looked at one another, uneasily.

''Yep,'' said Krass, his body beginning to sway a bit, ''good thing we didn't get to the party later. Coulda been us that got ate. Or worse, coulda been me!''

''Come on now, Bryant,'' said Tate. ''We came here to have a good time and forget what happened four nights ago, not start talking about it and getting all depressed all over again. What's happened is over and there's no further mystery about it.''

''Maybe. Maybe not.'' Krass' hands vibrated, long fingers enwrapping the whiskey bottle like the legs of some fleshy arthropod. He looked at Richard Kessler's face and was amused to see it flush pink.

"And let's not forget about dear ol' Bugs."

He could see the reactions that suddenly appeared on the five distorted faces. Reactions of guilt that elicited another smile on Krass' face.

"I, uh, think it's getting late," said Dr. Bertrand. His right cheek began to twitch beneath the thick lens of his spectacles. "And I, for one, have to get an early start in the morning. I'm preparing a new exhibit at the museum. And as we say in the paleo department, *Meganeura monyi* will not wait for ex-fraternity brothers with hangovers."

Krass wasn't listening; he was enjoying the way the five men squirmed in their chairs, all because he had the gall to speak about something other than their trivial memories. The nostalgia of enjoying another beer fest at Kelly's, just like "in the good old days," had been abruptly smashed.

"Besides," said the major, "I have grown accustomed to fine foods and this cheap beer is giving me a severe stomach ache."

"I don't feel as great as I did when I came here twenty-five years ago either," said Tate.

"Neither do I," said Lance. "I think we're all a little out of condition."

"We've got to get together again sometime," said Tate. "Right here at Kelly's. Soon."

"Agreed," said Dr. Bertrand. "It's certainly been enjoyable."

Four of the group stood to leave. Bryant Krass remained seated, still leering, still clutching his bottle of whiskey. Also sitting at the table was Richard Kessler, seemingly frozen to his chair. Kessler's eyes were frozen wide with terror, his body rigid as stone. Only his right hand revealed any movement of his body. It was vibrating as though he were about to suffer a nervous breakdown.

"What the hell's wrong with you?" asked Krass. "You seen a ghost or something?"

Kessler did not reply. He only continued to shake his hand. With apparently excrutiating effort he extended his index finger. Pointed . . .

Krass stared until he could see the blurry image of something waiting motionless on the left edge of the table. Something small, its dark body almost invisible against the brown table. Something covered by an almost obscene layer of coarse fur. Something with eyes like four glossy balls of black glass. Glaring eyes.

There was movement at Krass' left shoulder. He saw Dr. Bertrand lean over him for a closer look at the miniscule creature that had somehow struck terror in the insurance man. The paleontologist's glasses touched coldly against Krass' cheek.

"It's nothing at all," said Dr. Bertrand in throaty voice. "Nothing but a small jumping spider."

"Why doesn't it jump?" asked Krass.

Kessler's lips quivered. His eyes remained locked in a horrible stare on the eight-legged creature. "But . . ." he finally managed to speak, "you must remember . . . that I've always had this . . . this thing about spiders."

"*Thing?*" said Krass. "Seems more like *fear* to me."

Kessler did not turn away from the spider, as though he were afraid it would move. "Ever since I was a kid, I've had this . . . I've been afraid of . . ."

"I may be a paleontologist," said Dr. Bertrand. "But I know enough about modern day arachnids to know a jumping spider of the family *Salticidae* when I see one. Believe me, Dick, there's nothing to be afraid of. This critter's quite fascinating, in fact. If you look hard enough you'll note four eyes."

"All the better to see you with, my dear," laughed Krass.

"And you better listen to Willie. He should know about critters with four eyes."

Ignoring Krass' words, the paleontologist continued. "I'd wager that this one's vision is excellent as far as arachnids go. He's probably as terrified of you as you are of him. Most likely he's just interested. At any rate, you've got nothing to fear. Though for the life of me I don't know what he's doing here at Kelly's."

"Don't you see?" said Kessler, raising his voice. "He's staring at me! *At me!*"

"Don't be ridiculous," said the major. "You're acting juvenile."

"Please . . . somebody try to understand. This is a phobia with me. Something I can't help. I've had it since childhood, when I accidentally stepped on a spider in my bare feet one night, in my bedroom. Then I started to have all those recurring nightmares of being the victim of an enormous spider, trapped in its gigantic web. Then it crawled onto my chest and . . .

"No!"

Krass poured himself another shot of whiskey. He gulped it down. Felt new warmth. A furnace deep down inside. Saw new distortion in the extreme. Saw the spider. Saw it start to move. Across the table. Toward Dick. Saw Dick tense, eyes popping. Heard Dick say, "Now! It's coming for me!"

"Well if that little bug's buggin' you," Krass said with something trying to hold back his words, "ol' frat brother'll fix it for you."

With that, Bryant Krass slammed his elbow hard upon the crawling arachnid, crunching through the brittle exoskeleton. The jumping spider wriggled a few seconds beneath the crushing weight and died.

"Well, there's one jumping spider that won't do any more

jumping,'' said Krass, pulling himself away from the table. When he sat back his head floated in a sea of booze. Then he clasped Kessler's shivering shoulder and breathed an offensive stream of hot, whiskey air into the insurance man's face.

Filling his glass again with the golden liquid, Krass said with an equally offensive belch, "You see, Dickie ol' buddy, now ever-body can go home." He downed the final shot of whiskey for the night and said with a sly grin, "Hey . . . wonder if ol' Bugs sent you that ol' spider . . . as a present . . ." Then he fell hard against the wooden tabletop.

Blackness came. When the blackness disappeared, Bryant Krass was walking. Not under his own power, but with the aid of a fat, lumbering man in an army uniform over whose sturdy right shoulder he was draped.

Shadows, created by barren trees in the light of a nearly full moon, clutched at the walls of a house. A mustard yellow house, hardly more than a shack, old and rundown. Krass' house, to which he always managed to return after his latest binge. To Krass the shadows were eerie creatures of darkness, tonight appearing even more eerie than usual. This was the worst he'd been in months and he did not fear the shadows. Why should he fear these quiet things that ever welcomed him home?

"All right, Bryant, you're home," said Major Alex Gear, "if this dump is really where you live. But I've seen better barracks than this."

"Thanks for the ride. Just prop me up against the door. Been through this all a billion times."

"Whatever you say. The fact is, the sooner I leave you, the better."

Krass did his best to perform a military about-face for the major's benefit. But Gear only snorted, then marched back to the old Chevrolet sedan that was parked on the dirt road. He looked back and frowned as Krass smiled at him.

"You sure you don't need any help?"

"Positive. I been drunker before. To me this is as natural as you gettin' up for taps. Or . . ."

Krass raised a wobbly hand in an awkward salute. It was as difficult to move as it was to speak.

"All right then, Bryant. Good-night. Perhaps I'll see you again if our group gets together again."

As the major drove away, nobody saw Bryant Krass attempt his final and worst salute. No one, unless those gnarled shadows who were watching saw Krass fumble with the rusted knob of the front door. The door wasn't locked. Never was. There was really no reason to lock it since he owned nothing that any thief might want to possess or hadn't already taken.

The house was as decrepit as Krass himself. It stank, not only of alcohol, but of filth and mold that had accumulated over twelve years of gutter living. Some windows were cracked, others smashed.

Usually there was something to greet him; something distorted and impossible. He had become accustomed to the myriad creatures that alcohol conjured up for him. Usually they were fascinating. He welcomed the pink elephants—even the pink mammoths that Willie had mused about back in college—for they provided some company in this dreary, lonely old house.

Krass smiled expectantly as he opened the door and switched on the dim twenty-five-watt light bulb. Ah! he thought, peering at the blurry green mass that stretched before him like a quivering, living rug. Something different for a change. He was, admittedly, becoming weary of the multi-colored pachyderms. How refreshing to see this carpet of green. Greenish creatures with cute little wings resting against sleekly elongated bodies. Ah, and they were waiting for him.

He stooped for a better look, his head swirling from the

sudden shift in altitude. He belched and tasted whiskey. His eyes started to focus again. Now he could better discern the appearance of the individual creatures.

For a few moments he felt like some herculean god hovering over his guests. And how these night visitors responded to their returning deity! How nice, the god comes back to his yellow church to find a green congregation with arms folded in silent prayer.

Burping, he moved still closer to his greenish flock. He saw that the church-goers were moving nearer to him.

"Good evening," he said with a grin. "My name is Bryant Krass. Wish I could offer you something. But unfortunately . . . the liquor cupboard is bare."

Krass extended a shaky hand and reached for the back of one of his tiny congregation. His mind spun dizzily, his head felt like swirling gas. Balance was almost impossible. Then he stumbled forward, plunging stomach first atop the waiting group. Only then did Bryant Krass realize that he was a fool to be smiling. At last he screamed. Unfortunately there were no human ears to hear him.

How long Mantis and his brothers had waited did not matter. They had remained motionless, resting upon their thin hind and middle legs, with their front legs raised and tucked beneath their underbellies. In the past they had waited longer for their food. This was in accordance with the Way.

The praying mantises hungered. Yet, had it not been for the Call, these great hunters would have fought mortally against each other, until only one—most likely Mantis himself, claimed this place as his own.

The monster that had tumbled upon them squirmed. Some of their numbers had been killed by the creature's fall. This only added to their anticipation of the deed that they must perform.

Mantis himself inched toward the writhing creature. His

forelegs were still folded, the strong external spines locked together like teeth. His heart-shaped head with its large eyes turned to view his hungry brothers. He saw them still in the same position that told him they demanded food.

But Mantis commanded the first morsel of the feast for himself. Thus, he released his message, letting it issue through the air until the others knew that they must wait.

Cautiously he continued to move on his four legs and then opened his forelimbs, the spikes parting like the jaws of some chitonous reptile. With incredible speed he thrust his front legs against the titanic victim, imbedding his spikes deep . . . deeper into the quivering flesh.

The victim shrieked.

Mantis retracted his forelegs only slightly, only enough to tighten his grip, only enough to make his grip more difficult to break. Liquid spilled out to drown Mantis' spikes.

The monster lunged. It flailed out with enormous forelimbs, slithering atop the crushed bodies of a dozen praying mantises. Its soft-skinned appendages flew about, splitting and crushing a dozen more. Internal organs oozed from crunched bodies.

But Mantis did not release his hold. For that was not the sign of a great leader. He only began to feast.

Then the others advanced, some lacking forelegs or even heads because of the monster's onslaught, and all demanding gratification of their insatiable appetite for mammal flesh.

The victim twisted amid the converging horde. It gave out yet another, louder, shattering noise. The mantises were already upon it in countless numbers, biting voraciously through its flesh. Biting and chewing and consuming.

Mantis feasted as he had never feasted before. He reveled in the awesome size of his prey, a creature he would never have attempted slaying according to the Way. But now a force he could not comprehend had roused him to lead others of his kind against so monstrous an enemy. Tonight Mantis was indeed worthy to lead.

He was grateful. Mantis enjoyed this delectable new food. He continued to chomp and swallow and digest until he and his brothers no longer hungered, and until their mountainlike meal had long since ceased to move.

CHAPTER SIX

"Look alive, woman! I'm home!"

Maj. Alex Gear, retired, stood in the doorway of his ranch style home. He loomed large. His mass—almost three hundred pounds last time he dared step on the bathroom scale—filled the black suit he was wearing on this Thursday evening. He would have preferred to wear his old army uniform. But the uniform fit him so snugly that now he wore it only on special or important occasions, like the fraternity reunion at Ronald Reid's home or the night before at Kelly's Pub.

He could see Florence peering out of the kitchen. The look on her face seemed to indicate a mixture of temerity and awe. Temerity over his imposing presence and awe over the amount of weight he had accumulated since she first saw him in his impressive uniform fourteen years ago.

"Who was that outside, Florence?" he asked.

Florence's eyes looked about curiously. "Who was outside? Why, no one, I don't think."

The Major wrinkled his mouth, then scowled at his wife as he once might have scowled at a new rookie in boot camp.

"That's odd. For a moment I thought I saw someone moving about just as I came up the walk," he said. "But I guess my eyes aren't as good as they used to be."

Alex Gear moved slowly into the living room, with its framed military citations and the large American flag that stood in one corner. He removed his black felt hat and tossed it onto the large dark green sofa. Then he sat down to be sucked into the soft cushions.

His head bobbed up and down, his eyes surveying his wife as she walked into the living room. She was dressed in her pea green dress, the one she'd had for a year and usually wore only when the Gears were having guests. As usual, Florence Gear failed to pass a perfect inspection.

"Confound it, Florence," he snorted, "if you insist on wearing a dress with gold buttons, at least have the common decency to make sure they're polished. Nothing worse than dull buttons on an otherwise impeccable uniform."

Florence self-consciously looked down at her dress. The buttons cast a yellow glow upon her face. "Yes, dear," she said timidly.

"See that it doesn't happen again, woman," he ordered with the resonant voice he had used on the men back in Korea. He didn t smile outwardly but inside he grinned wide as his belly. There was no doubt in his mind as to the way his commands should be received. Obedience, he thought. There must be obedience, immediately and unquestioningly, to smoothly run an army or household. "Confound it, woman! Must I always keep watch over you?"

Gear puffed out his round cheeks much as he had done during his war days, when his cheeks weren't quite so round. In those years his commands really meant something. His voice made even the roughest soldiers just off the slum streets or out of the prize rings, tremble. His words could move great troops of armed soldiers or start the engines of monstrous tanks. Now, whom did he have to obey his orders? No one but one husky, middle-aged woman wearing an ill-fitting dress and a string of artificial pearls.

He raised his head. His nostrils sniffed at a pleasant aroma that drifted in from the kitchen. As he breathed deeply of the scent, the major smiled. Wrinkling his pudgy nose, he remained silent until he was certain as to the nature of the odors.

Ah! he thought. Garlic and warm butter.

Gear began to salivate and licked his teeth. He breathed deeper, trying to separate one ambrosial fragrance from the other. Already there was a simulation of taste in his watering mouth.

He leaned back on the sofa, which was sturdily built and could easily sustain his weight. His head snapped toward Florence with military precision. Florence stood there, as tall as he had trained her to stand, looking at him like someone awaiting a subsequent command. The major's eyes gazed beyond the green dress and saw her only as the creator of the gourmet's feast that she had better have prepared for him. She was, in fact, a fabulous cook. Perhaps this sole talent was the reason the major married her thirteen years past.

The major smacked his lips loudly in anticipation of the culinary delights that he knew were to come.

"Lobster," he pronounced. "I would say that you have prepared me a lobster. And I'd also guess that the aroma of garlic mingled with the savory smell of hot butter could only be the sauce for the most pleasurable side-order you have prepared for me in the thirteen year stint of our marriage." He raised his gray eyebrows.

A smile formed on Florence's face as though she were enjoying the major's basking in the aroma of her cooking. And the major knew that his compliments pleased her. This was the least he could do for so loyal and loving a wife.

Opening his mouth, the major flicked his tongue against the left end of his upper lip. He felt the smooth hairs of his thick mustache. Then he twirled both ends of his mustache and released them to stand out in space as if at attention.

"And *what* a side order you have prepared, my good woman! The aroma betrays its identity. What can it be other than my favorite *escargot?*"

"Just the way you like them," said Florence.

The way he liked them! Snails, served in their shells with a hot butter and garlic sauce. What could be more accurately labeled the food of the gods or generals than *escargot?* How unfortunate that Florence, though she could keep any gourmet ecstatic with her art, could not stomach much of what she created for her husband. A pity, he thought, that she would eat something simpler in the kitchen, something no more exotic than a reheated roast beef.

But he knew how nauseous she would become whenever her devotion to him necessitated that she immerse the squirming lobster face down into the scalding, boiling water, and watch it die. Then she must crack its hard shell open so that he could feast upon its meat, savoring every morsel. He knew that she preferred the solace of the kitchen to watching him hold the spear-like *hors d'oeuvre* fork in his stubby fingers and jab the inside of the snails and suck them delightedly into his mouth. She was overly squeamish and had the taste of an American schoolgirl. But her loss was his gain in an extra helping or two of lobster and snails.

Florence was looking at the major, almost daydreaming.

"Confound it, woman!" he barked. "Why are you standing there gawking at me? Can't you see that it's six o'clock, dinner time, and that I can't endure the torture of these aromas any longer?''

''I'm . . . I'm sorry, Alex.''

''Sorry? *Sorry?*'' He was becoming overwrought so that his face flushed as red as the lobster he was planning to devour.

''Please, Alex. Please don't shout at me.'' She began to weep.

The major's round cheeks inflated like some great factory whose boiler was on the verge of exploding. ''Don't please *me*, woman.'' Slowly he arose and walked toward the dinner table upon which his plate, silverware and a brass candelabra with three white candles had been previously laid. ''There's no excuse for such inefficiency. I've never tolerated tardiness in my entire career. Why, every cook I ever had in the Army brought me my food the moment he noticed that I detected its aroma.''

Florence did not answer, but she was mumbling to herself as she shuffled out of the dining room and disappeared into the kitchen doorway. The major listened and could hear her fumbling with pot lids, and the large serving tray. He grinned for he knew that it was good to drill her now and then, keeping her in tip-top shape. Perhaps next time she wore that green dress, the buttons would be as shiny as the medals on his uniform.

But even as the major dwelled on his dominance over his shaken wife and let his mind drift as though weightless with the smells of lobster and *escargot,* he did not know of the army that had assembled outside his home.

The army was organized, but its black warriors were nearly invisible in the darkness. Thousands of ebony soldiers moved speedily on legs like filaments. The soldiers kept close together so that their ranks moved like a flowing black serpent, toward the first level of perpendicular layers of light-colored stone.

Eciton was the general of this black army.

His warriors were predators, usually content with the food provided by small animals, or even eight-legged creatures similar to themselves, some of which often fought back with additional legs fortified with snapping pincer claws. But now they hungered for something different. Each of them moved on six rapid legs. Upon each black head, three simple eyes and two compound eyes gazed upon the first obstacle in their mission, that porous slab of stone.

The first to scrabble the slab was Eciton himself. He gripped the wall of stone, then without retarding his speed, scrambled onto another flat area as smooth as the wall itself. He continued to climb up other walls and along other plateaus. There was no need to look back at his warriors. For what could they do other than obey?

The army followed. They moved in a black stream until they had scrambled to the uppermost plateau. There they discovered another wall, this one made of wood and gradually becoming a web of strong mesh. A hole in the mesh, through which a bright light shone, provided them with an entrance.

Eciton was the first to enter the enclosure. He paused, his head swiveling slightly upon his black neck. There was an enormous creature lumbering about the place, moving erratically and carrying objects of gleaming silver in its hands. Its movements were not governed by confidence as were those of Eciton and his army.

Where to move next?

Eciton told them.

Up.

They must ascend the steep yet small trees of sleek wood that supported another plateau overhead. The plateau cast a great shadow over the smooth surface upon which they now stood.

As always, Eciton moved first. He climbed one of the four

wooden trees, followed by a thin river of black life. Eciton emerged atop the plateau, then proceeded to the great oval platform that gleamed like purest silver. Crawling onto the slippery platform, Eciton was followed by the others, taking their positions about the carcass of a creature that would have been more to their tastes according to the Way.

A great shadow suddenly fell upon Eciton and his thousands of soldiers. The giant creature loomed over them but, miraculously, did not gaze directly in their direction. Its movements were still fitful, almost unplanned.

Then the world was snuffed into total darkness.

When Florence Gear returned to the dining room, letting the kitchen door swing closed behind her, she was holding the expensive serving tray that the major had bought her for their first anniversary.

The major sat in the comfortable cushioned chair at the head of the dining table. He looked up, more aroused by the increased aroma than by the sound of the kitchen door. His eyes widened with anticipation, not over the return of his wife but of the silver tray in her hands.

He breathed deeply and sighed. "Ahhh . . ." he drooled, "I can taste it already. Tell me, woman, how long has it been since you prepared *escargot?* One month or two? Too long, I would say!"

Florence walked to the dining table without saying a word. She waited, as if for another command.

"Now what are you waiting for, woman?" he growled. "Just set the tray down in front of me and be done with it. Then if you can't appreciate the finer foods of life, you can march back to the kitchen and eat your bologna sandwich or whatever other excuse for food you'll undoubtedly fix for youself. And be careful not to spill anything."

Florence obeyed the major's orders with precision. The tray

wobbled in her slightly shaking hands as she set it down before him. Then she proceeded to light a match and set the wicks of the three candles aflame. Their flickering light created shadows and caused the tray to seemingly move.

Major Alex Gear grabbed the *hors d'oeuvre* fork with greedy anticipation. He snapped his eyes in Florence's direction, which was the only order he needed to dismiss her and send her scurrying back to the kitchen. Now the major was alone with his gourmet's delight. He could dine uninterrupted by his wife's trivial prattle, most of which he had stifled years ago. Yes, it was for the best that Florence did not share his tastes.

As always, he sniffed the air two or three more times before finally lifting the tray and beholding his treasure. This prolonged the ecstasy. Eating to him was a science involving several sensory steps, the first of which was smell.

Slowly, ever so slowly so as not to unnecessarily hasten the procedure, the major wrapped the chubby fingers of his left hand about the silver handle of the tray cover. His other hand still held the fork. Thrusting his head back and closing his eyes he raised the lid, releasing an even stronger fragrance. Ah! smelling was indeed an art.

Sight was the second stage of enjoyment.

Clutching the fork tighter as if it were a spear, he brought it down toward the tray, at the same time opening his eyes. He anticipated the assortment of snails that had been set in a circle about the boiled lobster. But as his fork touched the first snail shell and began to turn it over, he saw—

Blackness!

Not the expected orange of the lobster, but a blackness that maintained the crustacean's shape. *Confound that woman! If she ruined my dinner—* But the blackness lived . . . crawled.

In a black flash the blackness was upon him. It enveloped the hand that was so precariously close to the tray, the hand that still gripped the *hors d'oeuvre* fork. There must have been thousands . . . maybe a million . . . of army ants pouring across his hand and wrist. He could feel them—their obscene little legs—feel the pain of their bites as they began to tear his flesh.

A pool of scarlet mingled with the blackness on his hand. Flesh began to disappear and reveal the first traces of white.

The major screamed. Most undignified for a man of his rank, he knew. But he screamed a second time: "Florence!"

Awkwardly, he stood away from the table. The pain was unbearable. Each rip and yank of each tiny creature had its own special agony. He shook his arm frantically, slamming it hard against the table. But none of the ants fell. Gear's eyes opened like eggs.

"Florence, get in here, woman!"

Florence finally appeared in the doorway, and he glimpsed the horror that suddenly twisted the features of her face. She screamed even louder than the major.

"Woman, please . . . do something! *Anything* to get rid of these confounded ants!"

"Wh-what c-can I do?"

The major shrieked and buckled forward as much as his belly permitted, in an attempt to keep the ants localized before they could move up his arm to other parts of his body.

"Anything!" he exclaimed, waving his blackened hand about insanely. "Can't let them . . . spread. Can't stand . . . the pain!"

Alex Gear, ex-army officer, felt helpless before this miniature army. But he would not succumb to their attack. He'd defeat them somehow—with Florence's help. Dear Florence! She always followed his orders, always did as he demanded. She wouldn't desert him now.

He saw her face turn pale with her eyes taking on a dreamy look and her mouth forming an insipid smile. She hurried into the kitchen returning seconds later, a heavy butcher's knife in one hand. The blade glinted in the candlelight.

"Oh, God! Florence—" he said, reacting to the weapon she held portentiously in a raised hand. "Not that way! Not . . ."

But there was no arguing with her. She had heard his order. *Anything!* No, she had never disobeyed him before and she wasn't about to now. She would keep the ants from spreading. She would save his life.

"No!"

Florence raised the knife high. Her eyes were glassy. The fatuous smile on her face grew.

Crunch!

The major screamed the loudest scream of his life. The knife had cleaved neatly through what remained of his flesh, chopping halfway through the bone several inches above the wrist. The woman's eyes blazed madly. Again she raised the knife. Again she brought it down with all her strength to complete the task, severing the black horde along with her husband's hand.

Gaping incredulously as the ant-enveloped thing that resembled his hand fell atop the lobster, he raised the bleeding stump to his staring eyes. A gurgle sounded from his throat. Pangs of nausea poked his stomach.

He heard his wife giggling maniacally, then watched her slip into an armchair. She let the bloody butcher knife drop onto the rug and then stared blankly out into space as though nothing had happened.

The ants were still moving, starting to crawl off the hand and to the round edges of the tray. But the major, though lacking a hand, was still the leader he had always been. Despite the fact that blood was streaming from his wound; despite his pain he had to subdue his opponent.

Though his vision was blurry now, he snapped to attention. His left hand grabbed the tray's cover and forced it back down over the ants, trapping them within. Then, his legs becoming wobbly and almost unable to support his massive weight, he grabbed the neatly folded napkin covering his scarlet stump. Staggering across the room he picked up the phone, propped it under his neck against his left shoulder, and dialed "O."

"Hospital," he moaned into the mouthpiece. "Emergency, please . . ."

As consciousness mercifully left him, the last sounds he heard were his wife's mumblings.

CHAPTER SEVEN

Karen was standing on the steps of her two-story brownstone home when Gary Rutledge approached. She wore black, as did Gary on this Friday morning of her father's funeral. He knew how heavily her father's strange death must weigh upon her spirit.

As he approached the attractive house and the young woman who waited for him, he recalled the telephone call he had received from her the day before. That was the first time they had spoken to each other since that other Friday night, when he and his partner had driven her home. Gary did not want to pressure Karen, so soon after loss of her father. Better let her make the first move, he thought. She knows where she can reach me when she's ready. And so for the next six days, he attempted to enjoy his vacation by attending stock car races and ball games. Finally, at precisely nine o'clock Thursday evening, the phone rang. The familiar voice on the other end gave him a sense of pleasure. She asked if he were able to accompany her to her father's funeral, he promptly agreed.

Now they stood before each other. Her eyes were sad and for a moment Gary felt himself lost in them. There was something about Karen, some apparent radiation of loneliness from her, that made her spirit even more desirable than her beauty. Perhaps it was Gary's own feelings that he was living an empty life that allowed him to understand the way she might feel toward him. At any rate, he knew there might be a bond between them, a bond that had been formed during their first meeting, transcending even the recent tragedy and the coming funeral. That bond, whether it was indeed the beginning of an authentic love or merely something temporary, did exist. And it made Gary Rutledge feel as if he had risen off the ground.

Karen and Gary joined hands and walked briskly down the street. For the first time this morning, she spoke.

"I don't see it, Gary," she said softly.

Gary wrinkled his brow, puzzled. "See what?"

"Your car. Or did you take a cab here this morning?"

Gary thought for a moment. "Oh, no, I don't drive a patrol car all the time. Come on. That's my car over there."

He pointed in the direction of a polished five-year-old white Corvette. He had owned it now for a year and had sunk most of his savings into the down payment.

A minute later, the white Corvette headed in the direction of the funeral home.

The funeral of Howard Barks was a closed coffin affair. It was a small funeral, attended only by Karen, Gary and a half dozen assorted cousins, aunts and uncles. Karen explained that she had not invited any of the fraternity brothers to the funeral because they had not been close to her father and she felt extremely uncomfortable with them.

By the time the funeral entourage reached the cemetery, a dark noonday sky with its bizarre clouds oversaw the somber affair. The great expanse of grass was wet and smelling green.

Crickets chirped as the minister spoke the prescribed words over the bronze coffin and then watched it lowered to its final place.

Gary was relieved when the funeral came to an end and he and Karen were again driving back through the city. He sensed that she was also glad. There was little conversation between them as he drove her home and walked her to the door.

Just as he turned toward the walk, she said, "Gary, I'd like to see you. But give me a whole day to get myself back together. Okay?"

Smiling, he answered, "Sure. I'll call you Sunday afternoon?"

"Perfect. And I'll try to be more myself, then."

"I'll be looking forward to it," he said, giving her hand a tight squeeze.

"Gary . . . it's nice to see you smile," she said, then disappeared.

Her beauty and warmth and loneliness on his mind, Gary did not go out to his favorite singles bar that night. Instead he stayed in spending most of his time either reading *Tarzan at the Earth's Core* or letting his eyes wander to his silent black telephone. He slept little that night, wondering whether or not his years of bar-hopping had come to a most welcomed end now that he'd met Karen. When he telephoned her at eleven o'clock Sunday morning, her voice was more composed. If this was "the old Karen" he wanted her to remain "old."

The "old" Karen spoke to him from behind her closed bathroom door at three o'clock Sunday afternoon.

"It's funny, really," came the pleasant voice above the sound of running water. "I never thought I'd be going out with a cop."

"Cop's fine," he called back to her. "At least you don't call me pig like most people do these days. Chauvinist or otherwise."

He heard her laugh.

Gary had arrived at the house where Karen had lived with her father with exact punctuality. His job had created his habit of arriving at a designated place on time. But his punctuality was apparently too early for Karen.

The living room, where Gary waited, was rather spacious and indicated that the Barks family had a better-than-average income. The furnishings were Mediterranean-style and included a massive aquamarine sofa flanked by two black wood end tables trimmed in gold as brilliant as Karen's hair.

Karen's face still haunted him. He'd seen her face before, enough times to have it permanently fixed in his memory. But where? A detective was trained to remember. But apparently Karen's visage had affected him subliminally.

He was also trained to observe. Alone in the room with nothing to do but wait, he watched and listened. The strains of a highly-orchestrated rock recording spilled at low volume from four quadrophonic speakers. There was a pleasant scent in the air —the wonderful scent of jasmine—blended with that of sandlewood incense.

Two items attracted his eyes.

The first was a white envelope on one of the expensive-looking end tables. The envelope was none of his concern but he managed to find it addressed to Howard Barks.

The envelope revealed a stiff white card with handsomely printed script, inviting Barks to attend the silver anniversary reunion of the fraternity. Gary sneered. Some reunion! A man goes to a reunion party to see his old friends and what happens to him? And now here stood Gary Rutledge, the investigating officer of the case, awaiting his first real date with the victim's daughter.

Replacing the invitation in its envelope and setting it back on the table, Gary picked up the second, an old college yearbook.

As he held the book and started to thumb through the slightly worn pages, it automatically fell open at a point approximately two thirds the way through, as if it were accustomed to doing this. A photograph flashed before him of some of the members of Howard Barks' fraternity. Some of them were immediately recognizable. But time had affected others so that Gary found himself reading the names below the photograph. Samuel Tate was heavier and Richard Kessler was basically the same. Howard Barks did not appear in the photograph for the caption revealed that he had taken it. Bryant Krass, here depicted as a clean-shaven and well-dressed young man, and Harvey Lance, young and balding, were virtually different persons than the men Gary had met. There was also a fifth man pictured, his round face grinning wide, his apparently light brown hair chopped to a crew cut. The caption identified him simply as "Bugs."

Odd, thought Gary. No last name. No name other than this obvious nickname. Without further deliberation, he closed and set aside the book. Finding nothing else of interest for the moment, he sank into the soft aquamarine cushions of the sofa. Almost without thinking he began to finger through the stack of magazines that were piled sloppily in a wooden rack.

Then Gary's eyes opened wide. Now he understood why Karen's face had seemed so familiar to him from the start. In a way they had met before. How many bottles of after-shave lotion had she sold him in the past? How many cartons of milk did she inspire him to drink? Tubes of sex appeal toothpaste to use? And here was that face once again, smiling from the cover of a women's fashion magazine. Karen was a model. And although he had not asked her what she did, he knew he should have been able to guess.

He was still looking at the picture when he heard her voice from behind the closed door. "Just another moment," she said.

"Let me just finish brushing my hair."

Gary felt as nervous as a high school kid on his first date. Certainly he had met beautiful women in the past, even on some of his assignments. But they had been merely that—beautiful women with nothing akin to the force that drew him to Karen. It was always the assignment that mattered, the job of being a policeman and a good one at that. He always worked to see the job through to its completion and perhaps, someday, to get a little notoriety. Maybe there had never been any time for relationships, for romance. But with Karen—

Just what were her feelings toward him? *You're acting like a teenager, Gary!* If a real relationship were to develop, so be it. He'd had his share of disappointments before, many of which began with situations as promising as this.

The bathroom door opened.

Gary heard a faint rustle and turned around. He was smiling as he rose from the sofa.

"Sorry I'm late," said Karen with a warm smile. "Hope you haven't been waiting too long." She switched off the record player. "I'm glad to see you're smiling again."

Gary delighted in the vision that walked toward him. Karen's trim yet solid figure was fetchingly revealed by the tight white pants and the sky-blue long-sleeved blouse that left her entire midriff exquisitely bare. The white and blue contrasted beautifully against her sun-bronzed skin, which seemed even darker in the bright daylight flowing through the living-room picture window. When she stopped several inches away from him he could smell the cleanness of her just-washed hair.

"You look great, Karen," he said, taking a firm grip on her right hand. "Now I know why I'm wearing a certain brand of after shave. You sold me on it."

They both laughed and Gary knew that Karen had managed to overcome at least some of her melancholia.

"Where are we going?"

"Hungry?"

"Famished!"

"Good," he answered. "So am I. And if you can go for some nice Italian food, I'll buy you the best damned pepperoni pizza those brown eyes of yours ever saw."

"You've convinced me," she answered.

Placing his strong hand beneath her long blonde hair, he pressed against her smooth back, leading her outside where the day was bright and beautiful.

The sun shone. Robins chirped like some feathered chorus, although he had never noticed robins before. There were flowers, also, of such vivid colors and fragrances which he never knew existed. A cool breeze blew against the couple as they walked, hand in hand, toward the parked Corvette.

Ten minutes later the Corvette turned into a parking lot reserved for patrons of The Villa Critelli. The aromas of tomato and Italian spices drifted from the screen door at the rear of the restaurant and merged with the smells of a cool and unspoiled day.

"My mouth's watering already," said Karen as she and Gary hurried around to the front entrance of the restaurant.

"Best Italian restaurant in town," he told her.

They sat at a corner table, away from most of the other customers, where a candle flickering in a red flambeau provided the only light. The soft strains of "Bella Notta" gave music to the place while the very mustachioed Italian waiter took their order in broken English and presently brought them a bottle of chianti wine.

They toasted each other. And as their wine glasses clinked together, Karen said, "To us?"

"I hope so," answered Gary. Then he took a sip of the dry wine. "So you're a model. I can see why."

Even in the darkness of the restaurant, the blush that suddenly appeared on Karen's cheeks was apparent. "Thanks, Gary. But let's just say that my kind of face is currently in demand with people who drink milk and smoke cigarettes."

"Do you enjoy it? Modeling, I mean. Not milk and cigarettes."

"I suppose," she said, peering at Gary through the light of the candle. "Mom passed away ten years ago when I was eleven. Dad tried to be both parents to me and did a fairly good job. I started modeling in my late teens—seventeen, I think—when I found out that a toothpaste company wanted a smile for an ad. I already knew a little about photography because of Dad's job. Dad wasn't bad off. But he wasn't rich, either. So my modeling eventually made our home look a little nicer."

"How you doing?"

"Good enough so I don't have to do any porn."

"Maybe I'm old fashioned," he said, "but I'm glad. And I'm also glad you enjoy what you're doing."

She formed her lips into a slight frown. Her nose wrinkled. "Of course there are drawbacks. I've worked fairly steady and had little time to do any real dating to speak of. And most of the guys I did run into were horny photographers who thought a fast leap into bed was included with my model's fee. I think that turned me into a kind of hermit."

They smelled the pizza before it was delivered to the table. Gary took the first slice and bit through the layers of pepperoni, cheese, spicy tomato paste and golden crust. He moaned as he nearly scorched his tongue.

"Should have let it cool off first," laughed Karen.

"I always do that," said Gary, blowing on the slice.

"Well, while you're letting the pizza get some air, you can tell me something about *your* life history. Like what it's like being a sergeant for the highway patrol."

"I try to do a good job," he answered somberly.

"Lots of excitement, I suppose."

"Not really," he said. "I was an M.P. in the Marines, first. Then right after I got out I signed up with the highway patrol. I guess I thought there'd be more excitement than there really is."

"You probably saw too many reruns of the TV show with, uh . . . Broderick . . . Broderick Crawford." She began to blow on her first slice of pizza.

"Maybe so. I think just once I'd like to be involved in something big. A case that would make the seven years I put into this job—including four years of schooling and one year probation—all worth while. But all I get are small-time holdups at roadside diners. Abandoned cars. That sort of thing. For a while I thought—"

Karen's reaction was enough to make him stop this course of conversation before it got any farther. He couldn't admit to her that at first he had hoped that Howard Barks' death might have been murder. Postponing his vacation to continue working on the case would have been worth it. But no such luck. He couldn't make the headlines by arresting Mother Nature for being in possession of an upset environment.

He spoke no more about this matter as he and Karen finished their pizza and chianti.

The afternoon sun was still beaming like a fiery globe in an azure sea when Gary and Karen returned to her house. Her face was radiantly alive. Tenderly she touched his hand, then switched on the radio station that brought a slow and sensuous blues recording into the room. "Would you like to dance?"

"Would I!" he answered. And so for the next twenty minutes, they did, awkwardly at first—then with new-found grace, whatever the recorded music demanded of them.

But such an experience required little to shatter—such as the on-the-hour news broadcast that attacked from the radio speaker.

The bass voice insensitively yanked Gary from Karen's warm arms and thrust him into the stark reality of a different and harsher world.

". . . At ten thirty this morning the body of Bryant Krass was discovered in his shack on the outskirts of the city. The body was found by a gas inspector called by neighbors disturbed by a peculiar odor emanating from one of the windows. The body was several days old and in such a condition that it appears that Krass was eaten by insects. Substantiating this theory is the fact that the victim's body was found sprawled over the crushed remains of several hundred praying mantises . . ."

Pulling himself away from Karen, Gary scowled at the radio speaker who had just ruined his afternoon. "God damn," he groaned, bitterly clenching his fists.

CHAPTER EIGHT

This was one hell of a Monday morning. It followed one hell of a Sunday afternoon. After leaving a bewildered Karen Barks, Gary had driven to the city morgue to see for himself the remains of Bryant Krass. The condition of the corpse reminded him of Howard Barks. Krass' corpse, which was mostly skeleton, had enough of face left to recognize. The sight revolted him. For the news broadcast about Krass' death had interrupted the dawning love he was beginning to share with Karen. Gary knew that such a tainted first encounter would remain in his memory forever.

This morning, Gary had gotten that telephone call from Maj. Gear, whom he'd met the previous Friday at Reid's place. The major had been recuperating in the hospital for the past four days and now, he had said over the phone, finally worked up the energy to make the call. Since Gary Rutledge was the investigating detective in the Howard Barks incident, he was the man Gear had tried to contact through the highway patrol. Informed that Rutledge was on vacation, he demanded and got Rutledge's home number.

Over the phone, the major reported what had happened on Thursday evening—how he lost his right hand to a horde of hungry army ants and why his wife Florence was now a patient in the same hospital's psychiatric ward.

Karen had also called Gary that morning, several minutes after the major phoned. She told him that she had a modeling engagement that morning. That ominous and unfortunately reminiscent radio broadcast had made her tense and apprehensive. He agreed to stop by the photographer's studio for her when her modeling session was scheduled to end.

Gary walked briskly through the white sterile corridors of the hospital. The air was strong with the disinfectants and medicine, so powerful that the detective could taste them. Hospitals were not his favorite place, especially with thoughts of insects attacking three men weighing heavily on his brain. Now, beginning the second week of his vacation, he was back on a case that had already exceeded the ordinary jurisdiction of the highway patrol.

When Gary Rutledge entered the major's room, he brought with him a long and serious face that showed the effects of a sleepless night.

The major lay half drowsing when he noticed the tall man wearing a light gray sports coat hovering over him.

"Sgt. Rutledge," said the major in a voice considerably weaker than Gary remembered, "thank God you've come. And thank God that I'm still alive and finally able to talk to you. My wife, sad to say, will not be able to talk to anyone for quite some time."

The Major's right arm ended several inches above where the wrist should have been. The stump was now covered with pure white cloth. Lifting his shortened limb, the Major indicated a small control panel at the right side of his bed.

"If you push that first button," he said, "you'll raise this bed for me and I can talk to you much easier. I can't do it myself. This arm isn't even good for a salute anymore."

Gary did as the Major requested and watched the bed as it mechanically moved so that the patient could sit upright.

"How are they treating you here, major?" asked Gary as the bed came to a halt.

"All right, Sergeant. It could be worse, you know; I can't complain too much. I've seen worse casualties during the war. Somebody has even been sending me boxes of candy here at the hospital. One of the old brothers. He didn't sign his name, though. I guess he didn't want to show up the others."

"Tell me what happened." Gary was blunt. "Everything."

The major told the story again in gruesome detail.

"And you have no idea how the ants might have gotten into the house?" asked Gary.

Shaking his head, the major answered, "None whatsoever. Florence is an impeccable housekeeper and her painstaking cleanliness has never produced a reason for calling an exterminator. I'd never seen an insect, not even so lowly a creature as an ant, anywhere in our house."

"Do you know of anyone who might have wanted to plant those ants inside your house?"

"Unlikely. Florence rarely goes out. And when she does go to the market or the beauty parlor she has trained herself to always lock the doors."

"Then what do *you* think caused those ants to do what they did?" asked Gary.

"I honestly don't know, Sergeant. But I am not a stupid man. I know that Howard was killed by insects. Then that uncouth sot Bryant was killed by insects. And then this happens to me," he said, lifting his bandaged stump. "And my wife becomes a blithering idiot! I don't understand what is happening, sergeant, but I know one thing. One such attack might have been a sheer freak happening of Nature—a coincidence—but not three. Not *three.*"

"Three members of the same fraternity," Gary added. An almost undetectable smile began to form on the sergeant's lips. "I suspected right from the start that some human mind might have been behind Howard Barks' death."

"But who? I can't think of a soul who has anything against any of us."

"You'd be surprised how many trivial things can set off an unbalanced person and cause him to commit murder. My partner was once on a case where a man killed his wife just because her poodle barked all night and kept him awake. We could be dealing with some lunatic or weirdo who was offended by something your frat did ages ago. Maybe some bartender who never got a tip the whole time your group frequented his place. Something like that."

"Then that means that the rest of the brothers—Dick, Ronald, Sam, even Harvey—are all in grave danger. Who knows when the insects might attack next?"

"That's what I'm going to try and prevent," said Gary. "I'm still on vacation and have plenty of time to work things out on my own, something like a private detective."

"You seem to have developed an almost personal interest in this case," observed the major.

"I guess I have," answered Gary coldly. "A couple of interests really." Turning to the door, Gary said, "Someone controlling armies of insects, using them to kill, must be a scientific wizard with a tremendous knowledge of bugs."

"You don't think that Willie—"

"I'm not dismissing the possibility," said Gary. "Who can say that a member of the frat isn't doing these things?"

"Then," said the major, watching Gary walk to the open door of the hospital room, "perhaps you'd also better consider

Harvey. Bryant severely chastised him the last night any of us saw that sot alive. Is Harvey above suspicion?''

''No one is above suspicion, Major.''

Gary met Karen at the photographer's studio; she was still wearing the tight blue shorts and the pink blouse with white flower print designs that she had worn during the modeling session. Gary grabbed her wrist, and said ''Come on.''

''Where are we going?'' she asked as he pulled her along and caused her to quicken her pace.

''To get some education.''

Twenty-five minutes later, Gary Rutledge and Karen Barks were walking up the seemingly interminable number of stone steps that led to the main entrance of the Marshall Natural History Museum. It was barely past noon and the sun bounced off the series of stone maidens that supported the stone cornice of the century-old institution. Walking through one of the revolving doors of the museum Gary and Karen glanced fleetingly at two African elephants and the skeleton of a tyrannosaur-like dinosaur that graced the main hall. Gary then acquired the necessary pass to visit the third floor of the museum reserved for research and not open to the general public.

When they stepped out of the elevator, they smelled that characteristic museum smell. Gary and Karen walked down the dim corridor, occasionally turning to see an office or library or a scientist or two laboring at, perhaps, some future exhibit. Presently they came to a shingle which read: ''Department of Paleontology.''

''This is the place,'' said Gary.

''Sgt. Rutledge,'' a familiar masculine voice sounded from behind.

Gary and Karen turned to see Dr. William Bertrand approaching them. He was wearing a white laboratory smock and was lighting his pipe filled with the same aromatic tobacco. The paleontologist gave Gary a firm handshake, then accepted the admission pass and stuffed it into the pocket of his white shirt. There was a slight flutter apparent on his right cheek as the bluish smoke began to twirl from the sabre-tooth pipe bowl.

"You don't have to tell me what brings you here, Sgt. Rutledge," said Dr. Bertrand. "I've read it in the newspaper. And I'm afraid I must finally agree that these attacks don't seem to be results of an ecological change or imbalance."

Gary's manner of speaking was coldly direct. "I came here to talk to you, Dr. Bertrand, because you are an authority on insects."

Bertrand's face twitch became more rapid. "By the tone of your voice, Sergeant, I'd wager that you suspect I might have had something to do with these attacks."

"Wager all you like, doctor," said Gary. "But, again, I didn't come to make any accusations. I just want some answers. I want to know just how a man could somehow gain control of insects to the extent that he could make them attack other men. Comic bookish as that may sound, I'm convinced that such a thing is happening. And maybe a museum is the right place to get an answer."

Dr. Bertrand cocked his left eyebrow and stared out through the thick-lensed glasses. "As I told you before, I am a paleontologist specializing in invertebrates. But if you want to know some specific details that are out of my realm of study, I'll take you to the entomology department. It's only down the hall from here."

The scientist took his two visitors to the far end of the corridor, then made a turn. A second turn brought them under a hanging sign which read "Department of Entomology." They entered a combination office and workroom, which held models and charts showing various insects, both interior and exterior views, and a glass cabinet with an assortment of insects pinned in boxes like a miniature museum exhibit. An elderly man sat at a workbench. He wore a rather old-fashioned suit and a green eye-shade and was examining a dead walking stick with a magnifying glass. The man turned to look at his visitors. His large hawk-like nose and the heavy white mustache moved as he regarded the three people now standing in his office. Removing his eye-shade the man smiled warmly.

Dr. Bertrand introduced the two guests, then said, "This is Dr. George Ankrum, who is curator of the entomology department here. I'm sure Dr. Ankrum can be of more help to you than anyone else, Sergeant."

"I'll certainly try," said Dr. Ankrum.

Gary told the entomologist brifly about the insect attacks, then asked how it might be possible for such acts to be motivated by a human agent. Dr. Ankrum thought for a few moments, rubbing his small chin as if to stimulate his thinking. Then he stood from his chair, walked across the room and motioned to the others to follow.

"There are various ways a man could gain control over insects, Sergeant," said Dr. Ankrum. "We are learning more and more about the feelings—or emotions, if you prefer the poetic—of insects. We have learned that there are ways to actually manipulate these emotions. For example, certain frequencies of sound can mimic the mating urge of various insects. By using that sound we could cause a whole population of such creatures to mate."

"Hmmm," said Gary. "Seems to me I once saw an old science fiction movie where they did just that with giant grasshoppers. They broadcast a loud artificial mating call and lured them all into Lake Michigan."

"Right now we're experimenting with different sound waves to induce feelings other than the urge to mate."

The entomologist led them to the next room. It was a large

room, at least a hundred feet long, dominated on one side by a large glass tank from which a cacophonic booming emanated. "But there is a newer, more efficient means of accomplishing such ends, better than soundwaves. Sergeant, have you heard the term 'pheromone'?"

"Afraid not," answered Gary.

"Then come here," ordered Dr. Ankrum, "and have a close look into this insectarium."

Gary moved close to the glass tank. There was hardly any light inside and so, at first, he had no idea what to expect. But there were noises like those made by insects coming from the tank. Next to him was Karen, tugging gently at his arm.

The tank contained the scaly carcass of what appeared to be a rhinoceros iguana. White bones showed through the reptilian skin. And crawling about, revealed by the sudden brilliance of a light that the entomologist flicked on, were insects, nibbling away at the lizard carrion. The insects were small, no more than half an inch in length; dark with hairy bodies.

"Beetles?" asked Gary, unable to look away as the insects continually ate the carcass of the iguana. He noticed Karen as she turned away from the tank with disgust showing on her face.

"Dermestids, to be precise," answered Dr. Ankrum. "Beetles of the family *Dermestidae*. These beetles are ubiquitous pests at museums, frequently attacking the exhibits like the ones downstairs. They like to eat through the stuffed animals. Often they'll come right up to this floor and start chomping on some of the exhibits in Taxidermy. Or they'll start feeding on the dead insects in our research collections. But we actually put the little demons to work up here."

"What kind of work do you call *that?*" asked Gary, his eyes focused on the activity in the insectarium.

"As you know, there are many skeletal specimens here at the museum, either mounted in the exhibition halls downstairs or catalogued and filed away up here. We've found that the simplest way to arrive at a nice clean skeleton is to take the remains of an animal, place it in a tank like this, then expose it to a number of dermestids that we raise right here in the museum. The dermestids will strip away the flesh before you know it. Much better to use than acids."

"Hmmm. Like insect piranhas. But what does all this have to do with these . . . these pher-o-nomes?"

"That's pheromones, Sergeant. You are witnessing the result of pheromones at work. The simplest way to define a pheromone is a chemical compound which one bug secretes and another receives, constituting a process of communication. Pheromones contain insect messages. One dermestid beetle can, for example, give off a pheromone that contains the feeling of danger . . . or hunger, as in this case of the beetles in this tank. The other beetles, after receiving the pheromone and its message, can act according to that message. These pheromones can be received over a distance of miles."

"Then you're saying that the beetles in this tank could be acting according to the hunger pheromones of one of them?"

"Precisely," answered Dr. Ankrum.

When the beetles in the tank no longer gripped his fascination, Gary turned his back to them to let them finish their meal in privacy. He could see that Karen was somewhat upset by the demonstration. Yet before he left the museum with her, he had to make certain that all of the facts were stored in his head.

"Is it possible," Gary began, "that pheromones could be made synthetically? That they could be used by someone for his own warped reasons?"

"Exactly. I see that you've anticipated what all this was leading up to. Scientists are already experimenting with pheromones for the purpose of controlling insect pests. They've done some remarkable things with certain species of moths, artificially inducing certain needs to their bodies."

"And once you've, say, made a batch of these pheromones, how would you get them to their appropriate insects?"

"Simple," answered the entomologist. "Releasing the chemicals to the air, spraying the ground, splashing them or merely leaving a jar of them open somewhere to get the smell to the proper bugs; any such method could attract all the bugs of a certain species for many miles. The combination of various synthetic pheromones could produce spectacular—or disastrous—results. If you've figured out just what kinds of pheromones will arouse just what needs in what types of bugs, you could conceivably use them for all kinds of purposes. I shudder to think of what an enemy power could do to us if they decided to utilize pheromone warfare on a grand scale. Perhaps fortunately, nothing so elaborate has yet been accomplished with the synthetics."

"Hmmm . . ." Gary remained silent for several moments. "Maybe. Maybe not. Doctor, I want to thank you for all the help. You may have opened up some new avenues of investigation in this case."

Gary, still thinking about what Ankrum had said about the military value of pheromones, shook the entomologist's hand. Then he approached Karen. "Sorry you had to see that business in the tank. I didn't expect that myself. But I think we've learned something here today that's important."

Pressing his hand against her warm cheek, she said, "I understand."

Presently, Gary and Karen rejoined Dr. Bertrand. "I think I may be on the right track," Gary told Dr. Bertrand. "Now all we need to do is find somebody who knows a hell of a lot about sound equipment or who is an expert with these pheromones Dr. Ankrum was talking about. At the same time you'd better try and think and remember if there is anyone out to get the members of your old frat. I suggest that all of you put your heads together and think back twenty-five years. With the way some sickies think these days, it could even be some member of a rival frat who resents losing an old drinking match or something.''

Dr. Bertrand's facial tic came to life now. He seemed to be searching for a reply when his office phone rang. The paleontologist rushed for the receiver. Gary's trained ears listened.

Gary, looking, saw that Bertrand's face had paled and that his right cheek was trembling more rapidly than ever. Bertrand's voice suddenly became markedly faint and Gary had to strain in order to hear him.

''But, you can't mean . . .'' said Dr. Bertrand. His throaty voice wavered. ''Listen I'll—'' He noticed that Gary was at the door listening, watching. ''Wait. I'll talk to you later, all right? But think over what you said. Think it over seriously. Goodbye.''

Replacing the receiver, Dr. Bertrand spoke from the office. ''I have a lot of work Sgt. Rutledge. So if you'll excuse me, please . . .'' With a forced smile, the paleontologist walked toward Gary and shut the door.

''I think the pieces are starting to fit together,'' Gary said as he and Karen walked back to the elevator. ''I'm wondering if our illustrious Dr. Bertrand is all that he seems.''

''But he went out of his way to get you the information on sound waves and pheromones,'' said Karen.

Gary pressed the black button for the elevator. ''I know,'' he said, ''but he could have been trying to divert suspicion from himself by being overly cooperative. By getting Ankrum to give us that demonstration, his ego could have fattened—revealing the secret to us despite the fact that he is the culprit. Who knows? Working up here and seeing those beetles in action could have given him some weird ideas. And that mysterious phone call he just received certainly didn't make him appear any less suspicious in my book."

The elevator arrived. The door slid open.

Entering the elevator and lighting a cigarette, Gary told Karen, "You know, you might not only enjoy the satisfaction of seeing your father's murderer brought to justice, but you might see a new Gary Rutledge after all this is through."

The elevator began its descent.

"How do you mean?" asked Karen.

"You'll see. But first we have another old frat brother to visit—perhaps the only one with a real motive for killing Bryant Krass. We're going to see the butterfly man, Mr. Harvey."

CHAPTER NINE

"It's Harvey Lance," said the man in the black toupee with a pout on his pale face. Harvey resented the way the detective continually confused his name. But he resented even more the line of questioning that he was pursuing. "And you have no right to come here and insinuate that I killed any of these men."

It was the middle of a warm Monday afternoon. The sun glowed sulphur yellow from a sky of purple smog. The blooming garden in back of Harvey's two-story red brick home was alive with indigo, emerald and cardinal splendor with matching fragrances. A glorious day, he thought. Much too lovely to be subjected to this insensitive questioning.

Scornfully he looked at the two young people who stood before him. First there was the tall Sgt. Rutledge, who never smiled and never warmed those icicle-like gray eyes. Next to him was the daughter of Howard Barks, so utterly fashionable in her tight-fitting shorts and blouse and with her hair aglow as if she were making a futile attempt to compete with the brilliant flowers in his garden. Karen Barks stepped to one side, avoiding a garden rake, as Rutledge continued his questioning.

"I'm just following up a possible lead, Mr. Harvey."

"That's Mr. Lance. *Lance.*"

"Whatever," answered the Sergeant. "But I understand there were bitter feelings between you and Bryant Krass."

Exhaling loudly, Harvey flared one nostril. "Of course there were bitter feelings between Bryant and myself. But so what? Nobody really liked Bryant. He was tolerated but not liked. We all put up with him because he put in all the requirements during pledging and initiation. He made it into the fraternity and so we were stuck with him."

"Yes," said Rutledge, "but didn't you dislike Krass more than anyone else did?"

"All right, Sergeant, I'll admit I hated that boorish drunk," answered Harvey. He felt his face change to the color of his favorite rose. "But I didn't hate the others in our group. What reason would I have to murder Howard or Alex?"

Rutledge paused for a while, thinking. Then he said, "You know quite a bit about insects."

Harvey raised his eyebrows and turned his head, as if he were reacting for the benefit of some unseen audience. "I know about butterflies and . . ." making an unpleasant face, "moths. But I could care less about mantises, ants and their ilk."

Harvey Lance smiled when he perceived that Rutledge's questioning was leading to a cul-de-sac. He felt a sensation of triumph as he watched the detective and his companion eventually walk out the white garden gate and vanish behind the high wall of perfectly trimmed hedges that concealed the garden from prying eyes.

Now alone, Harvey Lance walked with glee among his many-colored friends. He paused at an abundant crop of his prized red roses. He smiled as he leaned over and inhaled the sweet fragrance of the flowers.

A buzzing sound blended with the gentle rustle of the wind.

Harvey turned to view with delight a black furry bee that hovered about a carmine rose. He had taught himself to know the tiny inhabitants of his garden by their scientific names, even though he was careful not to mention this to the sergeant. As he observed the buzzing insect fly away, he mentally noted: *Xylocopa violacea.*

The area was serene with the sounds of birds chorusing a pleasant music. What majesty! And all within the confines of his wall of deep green hedges. He filled his lungs with a deep breath that he pretended was pure, and returned to the house. There he rubbed his eyes, which were weary from the contact lenses that he rarely removed. Putting on his white satin smoking jacket with the initials "HL" embroidered over his left breast pocket, he slid gracefully into the opulent comfort of his very expensive sofa.

The blue French telephone, on the glass end table, began to ring. Anxiously Harvey brought the receiver to his ear.

"Yes?" said Harvey melodiously.

"Harvey?" said the voice. "This is Sam Tate."

"Oh."

"You sound disappointed."

"No," replied Harvey. "I was expecting someone else."

"I'll be quick about this, Harvey. You've undoubtedly heard about Bryant and Alex."

"I heard. But to be honest, I can't say I'm shedding too many tears over Bryant."

"Regardless, Harvey," said Tate, "I think I'm onto something. I think that we are all in terrible danger and that the reason for it is Bugs."

"Bugs?" said Harvey quizzically. "Bugs. Oh, yes, Bugs. Funny. I thought we'd heard the last of that over twenty-five years ago. When Bryant mentioned it back at Kelly's, I almost didn't remember."

"Bugs could be the one responsible for these deaths."

"Oh, come now, Sam. That happened so long ago that it's mostly forgotten. Besides, he was never one to hold a grudge for a day, let alone for twenty-five years. I mean really now! I don't have a better explanation for these deaths but I do think you're just becoming sentimental about your old days with the detective agency. I've got a sneaking feeling that you're just trying to put together a plot for a new mystery novel. Now if you'll excuse me, I am expecting a call."

Hanging up the receiver, Harvey gazed down at the large rectangular coffee table set before him on his genuine Persian rug. The coffee table was actually a showcase for what Harvey liked to regard as the finest *Lepidoptera* collection in the state. The lifeless butterflies pressed beneath the glass were truly magnificent. There was a perfect specimen of *Maculinea* with its blue and white spotted wings, augmented with black dots and trimmed with a fuzzy white border; *Lycauna phlaeas* with its gorgeous orange black-dotted wings; and the exquisite *Aporia cratagi* with black veins webbing otherwise pure white wings. There were four dozen other butterflies arranged like a museum display beneath the protective glass.

The living room of Harvey's smartly furnished home was a veritable *Lepidoptera* museum in itself. The ashtrays and drinking glass coasters each contained a colorful butterfly which he had captured in his own net and had gone to the expense to preserve while he, unfortunately, grew older. Butterflies provided the basic design for the house's interior decoration. They appeared in the wood carvings about the fireplace, in a splendid oil painting hanging on the wall in tribute to the blue-winged *Cedrocella* of Europe, and even on the small embroidered insignia that enclosed the "HL" of his smoking jacket.

For several moments he sat back and relaxed, feeling a surge of youth in his aging bones. While he daily found a new wrinkle added or an old hair gone, his butterflies never aged. He could look at their unchanging beauty and pretend that he was also remaining the same.

Despite the completeness of Harvey's collection, he never avoided the possibility of acquiring some new addition. He saw his collection as perpetually in flux, always growing, and he endeavored to obtain any new specimen that might fly into his waiting net. That is why the collector's eyes bulged as he perceived what was fluttering into his open window.

Harvey Lance's eyes focused hard through the uncomfortable contact lenses. His lower jaw dropped open a few inches. There could be no mistake in his identification of the creature. No, impossible though it seemed, there could be no error.

It was a stunning example of *Papilio demetrius,* a regal swallowtail with swirls of rich orange adorning the curvy projections of the back wings. The orange glowed in the radiance of the afternoon sun. As the wings continued to flutter, the butterfly did not return to the flowers from where it must have come. Rather, it stayed hovering in the air, framed by the open window, as though beckoning to Harvey.

But how could this be? Harvey knew well his *Lepidoptera* lore and wondered why *Papilio demetrius* should be flapping about his window. This particular butterfly was indigenous to the tropics, not here. But he wasn't mistaken. He had seen enough specimens of this swallowtail in museums and pictured in books to know the species.

Briefly he thought he heard the sound of his garden gate closing. But all that concerned Harvey Lance was the butterfly in his window. "Stay right where you are," he whispered, "because you're going to make my collection a trifle more complete. I don't know how you got here, but here, I hope you'll stay."

Smoothly Harvey rose from his couch and reached for the butterfly net that rested against the wall. He always kept the net where it could easily be grabbed in the event of such a discovery as this. His fingers grasped firmly the metal pole of the net. He didn't bother removing the smoking jacket as there was no guaranteeing how long the swallowtail would remain flapping in his window.

Creeping across the living room, net held tightly, Harvey said in whisper, "Now don't go anywhere." Ever so slowly he raised the metal pole. Harvey's eyes widened with anticipation, and he licked his lips nervously. He had made difficult snatches before but this one seemed embarrassingly simple. *Now!* Harvey swung the pole, bringing the net within the area of space occupied by the swallowtail.

"Darn!" his deep voice groaned.

The swallowtail was no longer in the window. Its flight was blinding, almost impossible to follow.

Harvey leaned out the window. The butterfly was outside now, over the violet-colored pansies. Still waiting for him? This time, Harvey swore, the elusive little beauty would not escape his net!

Moments passed he was in the garden, his satin smoking jacket brightly reflecting the brilliance of the sun. The swallowtail had not yet moved from its hovering position but something had changed. The tweeting of birds that Harvey had heard only minutes before had been replaced by the buzzes of bees and the chirruping of any numbers of other species of insect. But Harvey thought only of *Papilio demetrius*.

Inching forward, Harvey lifted the net a foot above his head.

The net cast a forboding shadow across the swallowtail as Harvey moved precariously close to his prey. This time he wouldn't miss!

Harvey swung the net, swifter than the first time.

"Darn again!"

The butterfly was now a good two yards away. Still fluttering. Still enticing.

Harvey muttered under his breath, "So you think you can play a game with me, do you? Well, I've never encountered an uppity specimen like you before. Maybe whatever it was that imported you into the United States changed you. Gave you some spunk to cope with this new environment. Well, my waxy-winged friend, your flightiness will only make my capturing you a bit sweeter. We'll see who has the last laugh when you're pressed under the glass of my coffee table."

He was no longer a mere collector of butterflies. Now Harvey was a mighty big game hunter stalking some equally mighty prey through the African veldt. His brow wrinkled; eyes narrowed. A look of cruel determination appeared on his almost snarling lips. Quickly, he closed the gap between himself and his winged game.

Again he swung the net. Again the swallowtail eluded him.

Harvey ground his teeth together. A deep throated growl tried to force itself from his closed mouth. He had passed beyond his point of endurance. The collector rarely became angry to the point of eruption. And never before had such anger been aroused by one of his loves.

Crushing roses and pansies and his favorite crop of blooming lilacs, Harvey bolted forward. Gone were any strategic movements. He saw the swallowtail and lashed out with the net, again and again. As the butterfly continued to flit about the yard, Harvey followed, angrily cursing with more emphatic "darns" than ever before in his life. He panted as he darted. Legs not accustomed to strenuous exercise began to wobble.

"Damn!"

The butterfly swooped across the lawn, flying close to the ground near the garden rake that Harvey had used earlier that day.

Harvey leaped, madly flailing out with the net. But as he struck hard against wet grass, hot pains spiked through his chest. He saw the dirt-flecked metal teeth of the garden rake, now ugly with blood, inbedded in his chest. Harvey's mind whirled. What was happening? It was almost as if the swallowtail had lured him out here to— Could Sam Tate have been right about what he'd said?

He tried to move but the rake-induced pain restricted him. If he could only yank the teeth of the rake from his chest. But every slightest movement to reach its wooden pole only afforded him more suffering.

What's that sound?

Buzzing.

Harvey's eyes lifted, vision obscured by the liquid forming there, to see the tiny creature zeroing toward him. The creature's movement through the air was swift. But Harvey saw enough of it to mentally click its name: *Apis mellifera.* Honeybee!

The honeybee vanished somewhere behind Harvey's prostrate body. Moments later an excrutiating stinging seared his left leg.

Contact lenses slid out of position in Harvey's watery eyes. But he could still see well enough to notice the black smoke twisting through the air, moving toward him like some dark tornado. He writhed but the impaling rake dug deeper. Now the tornado was only yards away.

Not smoke! he gasped. Honeybees! Hundreds of honeybees with only one possible target!

Pain multiplied a thousandfold ripped his legs. Harvey felt his blood pour, felt stingers inject their torments deep into his flesh. All the while the garden rake pressed deeper . . . deeper into his chest. Anything was better than this agony, even death. He knew that he soon would die at the rate his blood was flowing. Yet still he lived, to see the next horde of creatures that flew in to the attack.

They were creatures like those he so enjoyed viewing under glass. Butterflies would perform the final violation, he thought. Butterflies with anterior wings colored like black and white marble, posterior wings yellow with bands of ebony. Large butterflies who now produced a portentious high-pitched wail that carried above the sounds of the bees . . .

No.

Not butterflies!

Moths! *Lepidoptera* that he would never permit to mar his beautiful collection. Foul mockeries of the butterflies he so dearly loved. *Acherontia atropes*—sphinx death's-head moth, capable of stiffening the sucking tubes that dipped from its mouth and using them as weapons of attack and then—

Harvey screamed as the moths joined the melee. First he felt their damnable wings beating against his head, continuing until the black toupee slid off his head and exposed his gleaming pate to the hot sun. He experienced myriad new pains that needled his flesh. His body twisted as the moths, vampire-like, sucked his blood. And as life oozed out of him. Harvey Lance considered the attack in all its grimmest import.

Moths!

Wretched and ugly moths!

Surely this was the ultimate in human indignity.

CHAPTER TEN

Dr. William Bertrand carefully dusted any fragments of stone from the slab of rock that held the fossilized remains of *Meganeura monyi*. The fossil was a prize for any invertebrate paleontologist for it was a perfect specimen of this most magnificent of all dragonflies. Rolling his swivel chair closer to the wooden work bench in his office, Dr. Bertrand leaned over the specimen, then glanced over to the large electric clock that hung on the wall.

It was three o'clock on this Tuesday afternoon, a full sixty minutes before the staff of the Marshall Natural History Museum left for the day.

He lifted his spectacles and rubbed his tired eyes, weary from yesterday's fatigue. His eyes blurred momentarily, then focused upon the giant dragonfly. The data stored in his brain mechanically came to the fore. *Meganeura monyi*—the king insect of the carboniferous period. During the coal age, this giant dragonfly soared about steaming, amphibian-inhabited jungles on wings thirty inches across.

Dr. Bertrand could feel the strain that was gradually draining his body. The news of the deaths of Howard Barks and Bryant Krass was horrible enough; and now Alex Gear was lying in a hospital bed *sans* a right hand. In addition he was still shaken by the questioning of the suspicious highway patrol detective and recalled disdainfully the upsetting telephone call he had recieved the day before from Samuel Tate.

The scientist was startled when the telephone rang again. He heard again the familiar voice of Tate. But this time the ex-private investigator sounded frantic.

"Sam," said Dr. Bertrand. "What is it now?"

"Didn't you hear?" said the voice of Samuel Tate. "Another has died."

Gaping with disbelief, Dr. Bertrand replied, "Another? Who?"

"Harvey."

"Harvey? When?"

"Apparently yesterday afternoon sometime. In his backyard. I heard it on the radio in this morning's news."

"We don't have a radio up here at the department," said Dr. Bertrand with trepidity creeping into his voice. "And I didn't have the radio or TV on at home last night."

"Willie, it was the same as the others."

"Insects?" asked Dr. Bertrand. He did not really want to hear the answer he knew was to follow.

"That's how it looks," said the telephone voice. "The young man who had an appointment with Harvey that evening found the body. It was in terrible shape, like he'd been attacked by bugs. Maybe stung to death."

"Stung?" asked Bertrand feeling his stomach suddenly drop.

"The coroner hasn't performed the autopsy yet, according to the radio broadcast I heard this morning. But the police who came to the scene said that they found a lot of dead honeybees lying about the backyard."

"There's no doubt about it, then," said Dr. Bertrand with his mouth close against the receiver. He looked furtively about his office to insure that no one was eavesdropping. "Someone is killing us off, one by one. But who? Why?"

"I've already told you my theory."

"You mean Bugs? No, I still can't go along with that, Sam. I fear you're trying to play detective again and you're letting your mystery writer's imagination inflate all out of proportion. That name is buried in the past. We all swore we'd forget that name and what happened. And now you have to keep excavating it all."

"No, think, man," said Tate emphatically. "Who else just might be able to pull such a thing off? Who else might conceivably have a motive? And what's most important, which one of us will be next?"

Dr. Bertrand's cheek fluttered and did not stop. "Have you considered talking to Sgt. Rutledge? He seems to be quite involved in this case."

"I don't want to tell the police until I have some concrete proof to substantiate my theory. And more important, for our own sakes, I don't want to have to tell the police just why he might have a grudge against us. We would all most certainly be incriminated, especially if he has more proof against us than I can find against him. As you said before, that whole sordid affair should stay buried."

The paleontologist heard that Tate was breathing heavilly.

"Then what do we do?" asked Dr. Bertrand, his eyes following the length of the giant dragonfly's wings. "Just sit around and wait to be murdered by a vengeful lunatic?"

"There's only one thing to do," answered Tate. "I'm going

to confront him face to face. And that is just what I'll do once I've gotten all the facts organized in my mind. I don't want to make any mistakes. Then when I have my proof and feel that it outweighs any accusations he can make against the lot of us, I'll see about calling the police.''

Dr. Bertrand hung up the telephone, then shoved the entire unit along the workbench until the black cord went taut. He wanted to push that harbinger of tragedy as far away as it could possibly go. If he was disturbed before, now he was shaking. His face twitched as though powered by some hidden electrical device.

He picked up his brush and held it to the fossil of *Meganeura monyi*. There was no set deadline for the specimen to be displayed along with the fossil invertebrate and plant exhibits downstairs in Hall 37. But he would attempt to get his coal age prize before the public before the week was over.

His brush hand shook.

Dr. Bertrand set the brush upon the table amid shavings and chippings of carboniferous period rock. Although the entomology division was some distance and several corridors away, he could hear—at least in his brain—the dermestid beetles noisilly eating away. Vividly he imagined his own body slipping into their tank to be ripped and gnawed right down to a clean white museum specimen.

Three knocks sounded behind him.

Dr. Bertrand's body jerked. Fearfully he turned around in his swivel chair, half expecting to see the museum's population of dermestids marching toward him for a late afternoon snack. Then the paleontologist exhaled with relief. For the white-haired man standing in the doorway was elderly Dr. Ankrum.

''George,'' said Dr. Bertrand, ''I guess you startled me for a moment.''

''Sorry,'' said Dr. George Ankrum. ''I just came in to see

how the old dragonfly is coming along.'' He stepped closer to the man in the swivel chair.

''Slow. At least slower than usual. But I still have enough time to get the critter ready and meet my own deadline.''

Dr. Ankrum noticed that his friend was shaking. ''You look upset, Bill,'' he said. ''Why, you're shaking like a leaf. Do you want me to get you something from the health office?''

Removing his coke bottle glasses, the paleontologist rubbed his red eyes and lost his thoughts among the myriad shapeless colors splashing in a black limbo. When he could again see the concerned face of Dr. Ankrum, Bertrand shook his head.

''No,'' he said, ''but thanks anyway, George. I guess I've just been working too hard and too long, I'm tired.''

''Why don't you go home early tonight?''

Again Dr. Bertrand envisioned the dermestids that the department of entomology maintained on this very floor. He thought of Howard Barks and his daughter's story that he was killed by beetles. If some human force had managed to gain power over insects, surely having a few hundred carnivorous beetles crawl from their tank and make their way over to the paleontology department would be no overly spectacular feat.

''That's a fine idea, George.'' Dr. Bertrand replaced his spectacles. ''I'd like to do a little reading about *Meganeura monyi* anyway and I'd just as soon do that in the comfort of my home.''

''All right, then,'' said Dr. Ankrum with a friendly grin. ''In the meantime I've got to get back to work and do some preparing of modern day bugs. You get right home now, before the business traffic gets too bad. And get some sleep.'' Then he disappeared out the office door.

Dr. William Bertrand dreaded every succeeding moment as he left the museum that afternoon thirty minutes earlier than usual. The familiar parades of ants ran along the cracks of the stone steps of the museum. Cautiously Bertrand stepped over every ant, careful not to hurt or anger any of them and perhaps suffer a fate similar to that of Alex Gear. Whoever it was that was sending the insects after the fraternity brothers undoubtedly knew much about their present whereabouts.

The Volkswagen ride back to his small rented home in a residential section of the city aroused the twitching of his cheek and the shaking of his arms and legs. Every fly that happened to buzz about the closed windows of the pea green car was suddenly a potential enemy, craving his flesh and blood. He parked in his driveway, then hurried through the uncut jungle of lawn, each blade possibly hiding some carnivorous insect predator. He did not breathe normally again until he had bolted himself within the house.

The sky was approaching dusk when Dr. Bertrand settled into his old fashioned armchair with a worn copy of *Invertebrate Paleontology*. A miniature blue cloud, smelling warm and sweet, puffed from the sabre-toothed cat carved into his pipe. The scientist felt strange as he proceeded to read the book. Until now the great coal age dragonfly was a specimen of prestige, the type that could really enflame a paleontologist's emotions. To his knowledge the dragonfly surpassed any as yet discovered by scientists, in both size and perfection. But now the prehistoric insect took on a new and awful significance! *Meganeura monyi* had become a type of enemy lurking in the mists of another age.

Dr. Bertrand hoped for a diversion as an excuse to put the book aside. Thoughts of insects, prehistoric or otherwise, gnawed at him. The diversion happened almost miraculously when he heard a noise coming from the basement as though something large had fallen over.

Setting aside the volume, Dr. Bertrand slowly walked to the door leading to the basement steps. There was no need to hasten the investigation of the noise. The more time he could expend before returning to the book and its giant dragonfly the better.

He had not visited the basement for a week. Consequently he could not recall whether or not he had left anything down there that might have fallen over. He flicked on the dim stair light, then proceeded to walk down to the first level where another door led to the backyard. Staring through thick glasses, he saw the section of the wooden hand rail of the lower set of stairs lying on the floor. The railing appeared to have fallen over. The place where the wood had split was clean and a pale shade of yellow.

Without further consideration of the matter, Dr. Bertrand grabbed the remaining section of hand rail. The railing was loose, wobbly. Careful not to knock that section of railing over, the scientist started down the stairs.

There was a portentious creaking underfoot. Then the wooden step moved beneath his feet, fell away. Almost instinctively, Bertrand grasped the standing section of railing. He tried desperately to stand on the third step from the top. But within moments that step also cracked. The pipe, still trailing smoke, flew from his mouth and cracked on the floor. He fell a good ten feet and slammed hard against the damp floor of the basement. The way his legs folded under his weight and the pains that he felt in those limbs made him wonder if any bones had been broken.

Movement sounded along the cold floor. The movement of many tiny feet.

Dr. Bertrand gasped. What had happened was terribly apparent.

Termites. Pale orange soldier termites, with enormous heads equipped with formidable black pincers. Snapping pincers. Heads with waving antennae, sensing . . . probing . . . searching . . . *finding!* The creatures were moving toward Bertrand.

The scientist groped for the side of the wall. If he could maintain even the meagerest grip between the bricks, if he could pull himself up, he might hoist himself to the top of the stairs and escape to the yard. But the pains in his legs had not subsided. Even as he attempted to pull himself from the floor, his legs collapsed. Perhaps he could crawl. Maybe he could stretch his arms enough to reach that top step.

The termites were still moving toward him, their crab-like pincers snapping open and shut. They moved rapidly across the floor, so swift that before their prey could touch the attempted step they were digging into him with their sharp pointed pincers.

Dr. Bertrand screamed, knowing that he'd no longer need worry about who would be next on the murderer's list. Still he refused to suffer so ignominious a defeat. One important truth that his studies had repeatedly affirmed was that Man, despite his short lifetime on this Earth, reigned supreme over the lesser creatures. True, arthropods had been on this globe since pre-Cambrian times, over a billion years ago. True, there now numbered more than 850,000 known species of arthropods. And true, these successful creatures could overrun the planet if not for Nature's own intricate system of checks and balances. But Man had always triumphed over the Beast because of an inborn conceit that he was superior to the Beast.

The scientist looked down to see the soldier termites as they pinched off particles of his flesh and dropped them upon the stone floor. Each time that they repeated the process they caused their prey to become weaker. Soon Dr. Bertrand would be too weak to reach that upper stair.

More termites appeared from the shadows. There must be a hundred thousand of them, thought Bertrand. They were a great orange flood of wingless assassins, all biting and snapping and letting their prized pieces of human flesh hit the floor before going back for another.

He screamed again. *God! isn't there anyone out there to hear me?*

No, the insect would *not* overpower the man! Dr. Bertrand somehow endured the agony and reached for the top stair, grasping the wood which he prayed would support his weight. There were termites scattering about the step, chomping both upon the wood and upon his hands. But determination gave him strength. And although his body was steadily becoming clothed in a robe of living orange, he managed to pull himself up and reach the back door of the house that led to freedom.

With considerable effort, he stood erect. A termite-encased hand reached the doorknob. As he turned the knob, he squashed the termites that had latched onto his palm.

The door opened and Bertrand could see what remained of the daylight. It was sunset and the last vestiges of light revealed the horror he recognized easiest of all. The creatures were virtually invisible in the twilight as they soared to the open door. They were mostly blurs of the blues and reds that trimmed their cellophane wings. Dr. Bertrand was certain of their identification. For in studying *Meganeura monyi* he also acquired a thorough knowledge of its contemproary descendants.

How many dragonflies zoomed toward the open door? Numbers no longer mattered. For as Dr. Bertrand attempted to shut the door his hands and arms grew numb. Termites clung tenaciously to his forelimbs. He was no longer able to grip the door. The scientist sank to his knees, the door still open.

The dragonflies swooping upon him were well named. They were fierce. Carnivorous. So hungry that they began to eat their prey without even bothering to land.

Dr. Bertrand's glasses fogged, then dropped from his face. Without his glasses he was almost blind. He could no longer see what tore at him and for this he thanked God. But he could still think. Man had lost to the Beast. And someday, in much the same way, the Beast might reclaim its world.

CHAPTER ELEVEN

The scream of anguish still echoed as the white Corvette braked in the driveway of Dr. Bertrand's home. The doors of the sports car flew open. Two figures, Sgt. Rutledge and Karen Barks, dashed through the falling dusk and toward the house.

Smoothly, Gary ripped the .38 Colt revolver from the leather holster on his right hip. The action was fast, routine. The two-inch black barrel of the weapon reflected a beam from the third quarter moon. With the frequency that the fraternity brothers were being killed, their human murderer might be in this house. And if that were the case, Sgt. Rutledge would be prepared for him.

The detective tried the doorknob but the door was locked. He had almost expected that. Maybe he could break in the door, but that would waste time.

Again there was the scream, shrill and blood-icing, carrying its message of horror and agony. The scream now sounded as if it originated from the back of the house. Perhaps the back door wasn't locked.

He dashed to the rear of the house. His finger was firm against the warm metal trigger of the gun—ready! The slightest provocation could arouse him to squeeze.

The back door was ajar—open enough for Gary to know that his gun was useless. Dr. Bertrand's scream sounded again from behind the door. But there were other sounds accompanying his scream. Sounds that Gary's experience in this case told him were made by insects. How many or what kind of insects, he preferred not to even guess.

"You'd better stay out here," Gary told Karen.

"Let me go with you, Gary."

"Damn it, Karen! This is no time for melodramatics. You stay!" Then without further speech or deliberation, Gary pushed open the door. The sight was appalling. He restrained an urge to vetch. Howard Barks and Bryant Krass had been gruesome enough for the detective. But witnessing such a corpse in the making was another matter altogether.

William Bertrand lay there, twisting helplessly, hopelessly. His body was no longer the color of human flesh. Rather, it was a bubbling scarlet mass in which an indeterminable number of insects swam and bathed and feasted. The paleontologist's screams were now mere gurgles through his own gore.

Never had Gary felt so utterly impotent. He was an athletic man armed with a loaded pistol. Yet what could he do to combat this vicious horde? What efforts could he employ to save this man—if indeed Dr. Bertrand was already within the realm of saving?

There was no need for Gary to make a decision. The bloody form of William Bertrand jerked in one final throe of death, then settled peacefully amid the tiny monsters.

"Gary," Karen's voice called loudly from behind the closed door. "What is it? What's happening in there?"

"Stay outside!" said Gary with command. "I'll be out there in a second."

Gary's hand snaked behind his back, searching for the doorknob. His hand slid about the metal and its sticky coating of Bertrand's blood. At last Gary found it possible to look away from the corpse. But even as his stomach churned, he saw that the insects satisfied with Dr. Bertrand, were turning in his direction. Crawling from the bloodied cadaver . . . Moving toward him!!

Wriggling upon his shoes . . .

Flying to his right hand . . . latching on . . .

Biting!

Gary moaned, fought to twist the crimson-slippery doorknob and get outside. But his hand, now in pain because of the biting dragonflies, flew from the bloody knob.

"Gary—" shouted Karen through the door, her voice wavering with trepidation, "open the door. Please!"

Conflicting thoughts beset Gary's mind. Karen was outside with only the wooden door barring her from this insect lunacy. Even if he could open the door, he would be dooming her. Karen's lovely bronzed flesh—the same flesh that had given him warmth, affection, love—would further cater to the insects' cravings. No, Karen must not encounter these monsters. If he could only warn her, convince her to get back to the car—

"Karen!" he exclaimed as the pain continued. "Get the hell back to the car and drive away from here!"

"Gary! What's wrong? Let me in there!"

Damn! Why won't she just leave?

As Gary saw the blood appear in droplets of glistening crimson while dragonflies bit his hand, his mind exploded with mad thoughts—images of his own death in the same hideous fashion suffered by Bertrand, Krass and Harvey.

He turned, pushing himself against the door. With his left sleeve he wiped the doorknob clean of blood. Smashing his right hand against the wall with a force untempered by the pain, he squashed a half dozen of the winged attackers. He whirled about and grabbed the knob with his left hand. Then without further concern for anything but saving his life, he yanked open the door.

Gary saw Karen's immediate reaction of horror and could imagine what ghastly memories had been aroused in her brain. He wanted to shout to her begging forgiveness for what he'd just done. But he saw that the expression on her face lasted only briefly. Suddenly her eyes snapped with realization. Perhaps she could not endure losing someone else—especially like this.

Karen's movements were fast. She sprang into action as Gary stooped to tear away the termites that crawled from his socks to his bare skin. Darting before the open door, she saw the creeping termites and hovering dragonflies.

The insects seemed to watch her. They moved forward, beginning to spill outside into the open air. One moment more and they would—

But surprisingly, the insects did not attack the girl. They were passing her as if she had suddenly ceased to exist. Instead they were again moving in the direction of Gary.

Karen pulled shut the door, crushing a good number of the creatures and trapping most of them inside the house. Then with a hard stomp of her hard soled shoes, she killed several dozen of the termites that were creeping toward Gary.

Gary continued to battle the insects that were on his leg, picking them off until his skin was free. He rubbed his right hand into the wet lawn, squashing the dragonflies that still clung to him. Wracked by pain, weakened, the detective fought on until his efforts and those of Karen reached fruition. Both of them gazed about the lawn where the rapidly falling night was creating darkness. And not seeing another dragonfly or termite anywhere, they walked toward one another.

"It's all over," said Gary, embracing Karen and feeling the way their mutual heavy breathing seemed harmonically rhythmic. Then he smelled the odors of blood and sweat that originated from his body. He pushed her away from him and looked self-consciously at his bleeding hand and legs. "I . . . don't want to mess you up anymore,"

"Are you . . . all right?" she asked with concern, her large eyes looking into his.

Gary was weak. His legs and hand hurt. But he could see that relatively little of his skin had been torn away. Only a minority of the insects that killed Bertrand had attacked him. Thankfully the blood was already starting to congeal. "I think I am," he said, shaking his head rapidly to regain his senses. "But I think I'll have a million little scars on my legs and hand for a while. At least I'm alive. And don't you worry. I've got a talent for recuperating fast."

He looked toward the closed door.

"But I'm afraid I can't say the same thing about Bertrand. That makes five victims in this case, counting Harvey. I guess I'd have been number six if it wasn't for you, Karen." He touched her with his clean left hand and watched her smile. "And I'm not even a member of that damned frat."

Gary lit one of his cigarettes and for once actually enjoyed the taste. He released the smoke from his lungs in a slow, smooth exhalation and let it drift into the night sky. "I'll have to call the local police about this," he said. "Maybe they won't ask too many questions about why a vacationing highway patrol cop is so interested in these insect murders.''

''Are you going to call from here?'' asked Karen.

''Hell, no!'' he replied gruffly. ''I am *not* going back inside that bug trap! We'll stop by my apartment. I'll wash up and call from there.''

Karen took his arm as they walked back to the car, giving him spiritual if not physical support. Gary noticed her sudden silence and pondered if she was dwelling on thoughts similar to his own. He didn't pursue his suspicions just yet for now he was concerned with whether or not Karen had ever driven a car before. She had and as she maneuvered the Corvette out of Bertrand's driveway, Gary saw his last sight of the doctor's Volkswagen.

The apartment building in which Gary lived was almost ten years old and marred by a large white sign warning potential tenants against owning pets or children. Gary's flat was on the second floor, third apartment to the left. It consisted of a large living room, a kitchen nearly as large, a bathroom and a bedroom. The furnishings did not match and the worn couch could probably be replaced with a newer one, if Gary would ever bother to tell the building manager.

''Make yourself at home,'' said Gary.

Karen sat gracefully upon the sofa. She looked at the issues of *Playboy* and *Argosy* magazines that were stacked casually on his coffee table. She began to browse through the three paperback books that were also on the table—*Tarzan at the Earth's Core*, *The Living Shadow* and a Doc Savage novel entitled *Resurrection Day*.

''Do you read much of these?'' she asked him.

''I guess so,'' answered Gary. ''They're reprints of old pulp novels. They're about real heroes. And heroes are things we don't have much of anymore.''

Gary walked to the wooden counter that separated the living

room from the kitchen, and phoned in his report of Bertrand's death to the city police.

Then to Karen, he said, "Now I'm going to take that shower. And when I get out and feel alive again, we'll do some talking."

The shower was more than just warm and wet; it was invigorating. As the perspiration, dirt and dried blood began to wash off his hairy body, he began to think. He remembered how his suspicions of Dr. Bertrand always outweighed his suspicions of Harvey. He recalled how, following the death of the butterfly collector, he was convinced that Bertrand was the guilty party and had decided to visit him at home, unexpectedly. His mind also began to dwell on the importance of this case. The importance to one Gary Rutledge and the opportunity it offered him. Presently, revived and robed, he joined Karen on the couch. The lights were romantically low and Karen was especially alluring. The detective had to force himself to talk about an unpleasant subject.

"I don't know," said Gary. "I really believed Bertrand was our killer. He certainly knew a lot about insects. But now where are we?"

"Gary, a lot of things have been bothering me lately. About this whole mess. I may not be a detective, but I still know when something isn't right."

Gary let Karen tell it, anticipating that her thinking would coincide with his.

"Till now," she went on, "only members of Dad's old fraternity have been the victims of these attacks. Nobody else, until tonight."

"I know what you're getting at," said Gary. He began to light another cigarette which again tasted as it always had. "Tonight those bugs attacked someone else—me. But what's so amazing about that? Those bugs were probably controlled by pheromones or sound waves to attack certain individuals. I just happened to get in the way, that's all. So I had to die too. Right?"

"Wrong! Don't forget about me. I was there when my father died. The insects walked right up to me. They even had a good reason to attack me, because I, just like you, tried to fight them. But what did they do? They just passed me by."

"There must be a logical explanation, one involving coincidence." Maybe they were no longer hungry, he thought.

"Then explain this, Gary. Tonight the same thing happened. Bertrand was attacked, you tried to help and you were attacked; then I came and fought them and they still ignored me. And don't forget about Mrs. Gear. It's the exact same thing."

Gary agreed. "That is weird. Why should I be attacked while you, on two separate occasions, aren't even touched?" He stood up and began to pace about the living room, noticing that Karen's brown eyes were following him.

"This case gets more confusing the more I think about it," he said. "Let's see . . . If the killer is somebody outside the fraternity, someone nursing a grudge, who could it be? I think we can forget that Dr. Ankrum character, even though he might possess the knowledge to commit these crimes. I'm certain Bertrand would have had some suspicions about Ankrum in all the time he worked at the museum. If the killer was someone inside the fraternity—after Bertrand, I suspected Harvey or Lance or whatever his name was. But now both of them are dead. Frankly, I don't have the damndest idea if it's someone inside the frat or out."

Suddenly Karen brightened. "Gary," she said enthusiastically, "let me play detective again. Because there's something else that's been bothering me. Something that's sounded wrong to me ever since it happened. But till now, that something didn't really register."

"And—?"

"My mind wasn't all together after my experience in the bog. At the time it all happened, I could hardly think straight. But now it's hitting me—hard."

"What?"

"That creepy butler," she said. "That Grollman." She shrugged her shoulders as she pronounced his name. "The guy who works for Dr. Reid. Grollman found me out there in the bog. He told me that he was driving in from the nearest store with some booze for the reunion and that he just happened to come across our car since the lights were on."

"So?"

"I was with him the whole time after that. But never once did I see him take anything out of the car or bring anything into the house. Not booze or anything. And still he continued to serve the guests drinks while I waited for the police.

"What I'm getting at is that Grollman never went to town for drinks. He knew what was supposed to happen to my father and went out to check. But he didn't expect to find me there. That's when he concocted that lie about going to town."

"So you think that this Grollman is the killer?"

She nodded affirmatively.

"It's possible," said Gary, "that Grollman could be putting on a dumb act. Let everyone believe he's a slow-witted brute when actually he's a scientific genius who has something against the frat. He certainly is a weird character. But I don't know . . .

"More likely, the murderer is Reid himself. He admitted that he once had an interest in insects. And being a chemist he could very well know about pheromones. But why he—or Grollman, for that matter—would be doing this is still a mystery."

Suddenly an image flashed into Gary's brain—one of Bertrand's green Volkswagen, its darkened round headlights resembling the orbs of an insect. A "bug," he thought. And he remembered the curious way Dr. Ankrum continually referred to insects in the vernacular as "bugs." There was also a third image, one of a pudgy-faced young man with a dark crewcut, pictured in an old college yearbook.

"Karen," he said, almost in desperation, "did your father ever mention anyone named Bugs?"

"Bugs? No. Why, what an odd name. Unless you mean the bunny."

"It's probably a nickname," answered Gary. "I saw it under a photo in your Dad's yearbook. I just remembered it now. It was a picture of the frat and there was this character named Bugs. Somebody who definitely wasn't at that reunion. Somebody altogether different whom I know nothing about and who could probably very well be our killer. Karen, you're absolutely certain that you don't remember hearing about a frat brother whose nickname was Bugs?"

"I'm absolutely positive."

"Hot damn!" shouted a gleeful Gary, slamming his fist so hard upon the counter it shook. "I think we're on to something now, Hon."

Immediately Gary flashed to the telephone, acquiring the residential numbers of Samuel Tate and Richard Kessler from Directory Service, and then producing the slip of paper that he had kept ever since the Highway Patrol radioed him to investigate the death of Howard Barks. The crinkled paper still bore the telephone number of Dr. Ronald Reid. Losing no time, Gary telephoned the three surviving members of the fraternity and queried them about someone nicknamed Bugs. He was not entirely surprised when all three of them denied ever having known anyone by that name, regardless of his mentioning the photograph in the yearbook. There was a frown on his face, a look of failure, when he hung up the telephone for the third time.

"That last one was Kessler," said Gary. "He denies ever knowing someone called Bugs. And he was even in the picture. I could tell he was covering up just by the shaking of his voice. But what can I do now? I can't force them to tell me? If I did, I'd be kicked off the force for police brutality. I want to help them and the damned fools won't let me. Hell!"

Gary turned away from the telephone and suddenly realized that there was more to the night than saving three damned fools who didn't seem to want to be saved.

CHAPTER TWELVE

He was already waiting in the hospital lobby. Richard Kessler could see him through the glass of the automatic door. It was late Wednesday afternoon when the nervous insurance man interrupted the electric eye that caused the door to open and walked inside the hospital.

"Sam," said Richard Kessler with worriment in his voice, "I got here as soon as I could."

Samuel Tate rose from the dull red plastic of the waiting room couch. "Thank God you made it here all right," said Tate. His eyes were open wide and red from what appeared to be a taxing combination of worry and lack of sleep. He grabbed Kessler's flabby bicep hard, wrinkling the flat gray material of his expensive suit.

Reacting with a puzzled look, Kessler said, "Made it here all right? What do you mean?"

Pulling Kessler by the arm, Tate guided him to the couch. Then the mystery writer and former private investigator looked about with suspicion as if to insure himself that no one was watching or listening. He also cast furtive looks about the floor, the magazine-littered tables, the windows through which the sunlight was shining.

Kessler also gazed about the place, seeing the white-uniformed receptionist at the information desk reading a paperback book. He could also see the doctors and nurses hustling about, carrying and wheeling their medicines and medical instruments down the halls and in and out of various rooms.

Hospitals. Kessler detested hospitals almost as much as funeral parlors. He imagined that he could hear the moans of patients issuing from an endless chain of rooms that stretched along the white corridors.

"Why here, Sam?" asked Kessler, straightening his gray tie. "You know I have a phobia about places like this. I mean, if you had something so important to tell me, why didn't you just get it over with? Over the phone? Or even at Kelly's?"

Kessler recalled the telephone call he had received from Tate an hour before. He had sounded almost frantic and insisted that an emergency existed and that the two of them must meet—but here, at the hospital. He also remembered Tate's emphatic warning not to reveal anything to anyone, especially the police. Considering the fact that TV news had brought the story of Dr. William Bertrand to an unbelieving insurance man that morning, Kessler decided to cancel all his other appointments for Wednesday and go to meet Tate.

"It's dangerous for us to stay in our homes," said Tate, still scrutinizing the corners and shadows of the waiting room. "But in a sterile place like this hospital, *they* won't be able to get us."

"They?"

"And after I tell you what I've figured out," Tate continued, talking fast, "we'll go up to Alex's room and see what he has to say about all this. I wanted the three of us to discuss this at the same time. But there's been some delay. The receptionist said that we'd have to wait a little while. But now that you're here, I've got to get this load off my conscience."

"On the phone you sounded like the world was coming to an end."

"It might be," he said. "At least our world. Like it came to an end for Howard. And then Bryant, Harvey and now Willie. And almost for poor Alex."

"I tried to convince myself that maybe . . . just maybe . . . these deaths were the result of some quirk of ecology. At least that's what I believed when Howard got killed." Tightly grabbing Tate's lean wrist, Kessler went on, "Sam, we could both die at any moment." He lowered his voice to a whisper. "Sam, last night that highway patrol detective called me. He wanted to know if I knew anyone who was ever called Bugs. I lied, told him I didn't. But he seems to suspect something. Do you think that he's really doing this? Do you think that after all these years he's carried a grudge and, despite the way he acted last week, he's been getting even with all of us?"

"It all seems to add up that way," said Tate in whisper. "He knows about insects and he does have a reason to resent us. And I can't think of another soul who might possibly be out to get us."

Rising from the couch, Kessler walked to the window, pressing his palms against the cool glass. Then he turned his head to see that Tate was also standing. "Sam," said Kessler, "if we don't want to be next on his death list, we've got to call the police—that young sergeant who is already involved in this case. We've got to tell him everything. About Bugs. About us. Then they'll put him into a prison or mental institution before he has a chance to do anything else to us."

"No!"

"And why not?"

"For the last time, Dick, we can't go to the police," answered Tate, again grabbing Kessler's arm assuringly. "We know who the killer has to be. But we don't have any proof. Believe me, I've been through enough trials to know that with the circumstantial evidence we've got the case would be bounced right out of court, leaving us even more vulnerable to his attacks. Besides, as I've warned you again and again in the last week, there are too many sticky implications about what happened over twenty-five years ago. We are all guilty of a punishable crime. We could be put in prison and be sued for every cent we own."

"All right, we said we'd never talk about that again, so let's drop it. But what do you suggest we do, then, if not go to the police?"

"I suggest we go out and dig up our evidence tonight, when we'll have the protection of the darkness. Get some solid proof."

"No," said Kessler shaking his head. "If he's really the murderer, as both of us think he is, we'd be fools to go out there without police protection. You won't get me to go along on this fool mission of yours."

Their conversation was interrupted when a man clothed in white seemed to materialize before them. There was a stern expression on his lined, chiseled looking face. His slit of a mouth hardened to a frown. He held a small yellow card in his hand. "Are you the men who are waiting to visit the patient in room 2E?" asked the doctor.

"Yes," was Kessler's polite reply. Then he continued, "How is Alex doing, doctor? May we go in to see him now?"

"The woman at the desk said there was some delay," added the novelist.

The doctor's face was blank of expression. His voice had an unconcerned quality about it when he asked, "Are you two gentlemen relatives of Alex Gear?"

"We're close friends," answered Kessler. "We and Alex used to be in the same college fraternity. We know him very well."

"Tell me, doctor," interrupted Tate, "is Alex improving? Is he in better spirits?"

The coldly matter-of-fact attitude of the doctor convinced Kessler that this was yet another significant reason to loath hospitals. The doctor lifted the card to chest level. "Did either of you send Dr. Gear any gifts since he's been here?"

For a moment Kessler felt bad. "I'm afraid I've been a bit lax about such things lately, doctor. No, and I guess I'll have to send him something today if I don't forget."

"That holds for me too," said Tate. "I'm afraid we've both been so involved in our own matters that we didn't think of sending Alex anything."

"Well, somebody has been sending the patient gifts," said the doctor. He handed the small card to Kessler. "Most of them were simply from someone who printed his name on the cards as 'Brother.' This was the card that accompanied the gift that arrived today."

Kessler accepted the card and held it before his eyes. The inscription, neatly printed in elite type, gave the insurance man a chill.

Good night,
Sleep tight.
Don't let the bed bugs bite.

Sincerely yours,
Brother

"They did," said the doctor callously. "They really did."

Choking, handing back the yellow card, Kessler said with disbelief, "What do you mean, doctor?"

"I mean just what I said," answered the doctor. "The patient is dead. The most bizarre death I've ever heard of. Alex Gear was apparently eaten in his bed . . . by bed bugs."

Kessler gawked at the doctor incredulously. He saw that Samuel Tate was reacting to the impossible statement with equal disbelief. "Bed bugs?" said Kessler, his voice louder than before. "But there . . . there aren't any bed bugs around anymore—especially in a hospital."

"Believe me, sir, they were bed bugs," said the doctor. "I'd seen enough of them when I was a child never to forget what they looked like. An intern heard him scream and when she entered his room and saw what was happening, she panicked. By the time any of us got to Mr. Gear he was already dead —mostly from shock, I'd say. We had to seal off the room until the exterminator arrives. The police have just left here, but they'll probably be wanting to talk to you in the near future, since that card was signed 'Brother' and since you two were in his fraternity."

"But how could bed bugs have gotten into Alex's room?" asked Kessler, eyes wide.

"The reason I asked you about sending the patient gifts," said the doctor, "is that someone had been mailing him packages of candy, boxes of cigars, that sort of thing ever since he's been here. Always the cards were from some anonymous 'Brother.' So no one thought anything was wrong when a very large special delivery package arrived for him this morning. As usual, there was no return address. What this all amounts to, gentlemen, is that someone mailed him a box of insects. The earlier gifts were sent so that he wouldn't suspect anything when the big package arrived. If you two have any knowledge about this, I'd advise you to tell the police right away."

After the doctor left them, Kessler and Tate remained speechless for nearly a full minute. They stared at one another then looked about the room. Kessler's body was vibrating fearfully as he wondered when he would die and just what fate the murderer had designed for him.

Finally Tate spoke. "You still don't want to go with me?"

Shivering, Kessler said, "*No!* Especially now."

"Then I'm going myself. As soon as it gets dark. And let me warn you again, don't call the police. Remember that you're involved in this as much as anyone."

Samuel Tate turned, then walked with bouncing steps out the door of the hospital. For a while, Kessler wondered what to do. He was certainly too shaken to attempt resuming his business appointments. The hospital was affecting him like a den of white fungus. There must be someplace he could go, someplace other than his home, where he could be alone with his thoughts.

Kessler went to Kelly's. The old table that the fraternity used to huddle about was occupied by a rowdy group of students and so he sat alone at the bar. For a while he stared into the foam of his mug of beer. And when the foam had long disappeared the beer was virtually at the same level as when the bartender had served it to him. The telephone booth near the restroom seemed to call out to him. For lingering minutes, during which he sipped his beer, Kessler stared at the enticing black phone until his mind nearly cracked. No longer managing to restrain himself, Kessler dashed to the telephone, yanked off the receiver and slipped his coins into the slot.

Several minutes passed before he finally managed to convince the gruff voice at the other end of the line that his call must be relayed to the vacationing Gary Rutledge. He hung up, then waited for the pay phone to ring back. When it did, the voice that spoke to him was resonant and familiar. It was the same voice that had called him the night before.

"Sgt. Rutledge speaking."

"Sergeant," he said frantically, "this is Richard Kessler."

"I recognized your voice."

As the juke box began to blast, Kessler had to speak louder and strain to listen. He was almost shouting when he explained what had happened to Maj. Alex Gear.

"Sergeant," said the insurance man, "I couldn't keep this all inside of me anymore. There are only two of us left. Sam Tate and myself."

"Two of you?" came the receiver voice. "I thought there were three. What about Dr. Reid? Don't you think he's in as much danger as you?"

Kessler began to laugh an insane laugh, most unbecoming to a business man of his stature. "Reid in danger? That's funny. Sergeant, Ronald Reid is the one who's been committing all these murders."

"What? How can you be so sure. I would have guessed that the murders were being committed by somebody called Bugs."

"Listen to me, Sergeant," said Kessler. "And please, don't ask me for information then I'm giving. Years ago, back in our freshman year at college, we used to call Reid 'Bugs.' That was a nickname we gave him because of his interest in insects. Ronald was somewhat weird. And we, being normal fraternity brothers, took advantage of him. Anyway, something happened back then. Something which could very well have caused his mind to snap. Something all seven of us were involved in."

"And what was that?" asked Rutledge.

"I told you not to ask. But what did occur was something we all swore we'd leave buried in the past and never mention again. Something we'd do our damndest to forget. None of us had seen each other since college. And when he sent us those reunion invitations I felt certain that Bu—I believed that Ronald had managed to forgive all of us. Obviously I was wrong. And now, after all these years, he's finally getting even."

"You should have told me this before."

"I realize that," said Kessler. "But Sam kept telling us all that we had no evidence against Reid and that any mention of the past would incriminate us. None of us could afford a scandal."

"And where is Tate now? Is he with you? I'd like to talk to him."

Kessler glanced toward the window. He saw the black night sky beyond the blinking neon sign that showed the word 'Kelly's' in reverse. "Sam went out to Reid's place," he said, "in the swamp. I guess it's the detective in his blood or something, creeping back into his system. He thinks he can surprise Reid by going there at night and get some evidence without the help of the police."

"And when did Tate leave for Reid's place?" asked the Sergeant.

"He said he wanted to get there at sunset. It's already been night for a while now. Do you think you can get to him before he gets to Reid?"

"I can try," was the detective's grim reply. "But I can't promise anything. Meanwhile, you go someplace where it's safe and don't decide to take a drive out to the bog. You'd only complicate things."

"No need to worry about that," said Kessler.

Richard Kessler drove home that night with a speed that, under ordinary conditions, would have made him fear for an accident. But now, as he pressed the accelerator closer to the floorboard, he could only think of returning to the safety of his home. He was driving crazily and fortunately did not encounter any police. Once he almost met with a head-on collision when a long black car sped toward him along his own street, just two blocks away from his home. *Was that a Cadillac? A limousine?* He couldn't be certain of the identity of that streak of black that had roared through a black street and was now somewhere in the darkness behind him. But even as he parked and stealthily entered his home he could not forget the near collision.

He was tired, flurried. The TV dinner he had planned to eat that night no longer interested him. His appetite was lost somewhere and sleep was all that mattered, a deep slumber that could transport his soul to some other world where Ronald Reid and the victims of his madness did not exist.

Walking to the bedroom where the window was still open a few inches to let in the breeze, Kessler shivered. The cold air only served to increase the shaking of his body. He slammed the window, then proceeded to search throughout the house, closing every open window and making certain that no insects were crawling about the floors or walls or ceilings or furniture. Changing into pajamas and leaving the bedroom light protectively on, he flopped back on his hard bed. Seven minutes later Richard Kessler slept.

And Kessler dreamed.

The dream made him stir, moan. It was a dream he had suffered before, a nightmare the origins of which lay back in his childhood and which had nurtured and grown in the succeeding years. As always, he dreamed of spiders, hundreds of spiders, of all types. Spiders with enormous bodies, crawling upon his naked flesh with their obscenely hairy legs. Hungry spiders.

He screamed from his dream world and into the real world, so loud that his eyelids fluttered open. As so often before, the dream lingered like a hazy reality, superimposed over the lines of his bedposts and over the designs of his crazyquilt bedspread. He was cold, sweaty, quaking from the nightmare experience.

But then he began to breath normally again for the dream had ended and never returned again on the same night.

But had the dream ended? Was he truly awake? Though he was certain that the dream had been temporarily driven out of him, there was something moving lightly across his body. He could feel it creeping through the loose fitting material of his pajamas. The sensation was more real than any he had ever experienced in nightmare. Kessler raised his head and looked—then shrieked. For, with staring eyes, he saw them, crawling like eight-legged tanks clothed in brown fur. Spiders were flopping up over the sides of his bed—*My God, I didn't look under the bed!*—and along his supine form, his legs and arms and chest. More of them appeared over the edge of the bed, dark and shaggy against the crazyquilt. Tarantulas with hook-like fangs portentiously open!

Something else covered him. He saw the diaphanous fabric that followed the contours of his body. The cold tenacity of the webbing trapped him against the bed. He writhed beneath the intricate webwork. The misty wetness felt loathsome upon his hands and feet. There was no question that he possessed the strength to rip those webs. But that required movement and he was too horrified to move. For the implications of the webbing overwhelmed him. He was entrapped like a wriggling fly awaiting—

Kessler remembered reading that the bite of the tarantula cannot harm a human being. Yet, the mere sight and feel of these repugnant demons virtually paralyzed him.

Tarantulas pinched at his body with their drooping fangs, forcing more screams from his mouth. But those screams were only slight when compared to the shrieks that erupted from his mouth when he observed the *coup de grace* that was materializing at the foot of his bed.

There were an even ten of the new arrivals, as far as he could see. They were smaller than the tarantulas, but their size was their least terrifying aspect. These spiders were hairless and their color was a shiny black.

Latrodectus did not understand the strange compulsion she had for the great writhing hill. But she did know that the attraction, which brought her and her sisters to wait in the darkness below and then climb this peculiar structure, was irresistible. Had Latrodectus forgotten something? She felt as if she had just mated with a male. And from the messages imparted by the others of her kind, she knew that they felt the same. Yet, she could not recall the mating. There was no remembrance of the courtship dance of the male. Nor did she recall the sensations at her sides, left there when the male would climb atop her and insert his palps into her. No, she remembered none of these wonderful things. Yet she and her sisters had felt that mating had just occurred—and, repulsive though it was, with the great shaking hulk over which they crept.

They had mated. This Latrodectus finally and reluctantly accepted. The force which had drawn her from the darkness below convinced her. And since she had mated . . . now she hungered. Hungered for the body of her mate. Craved to fill her belly with the meat of her lover. Yearned for that necessary sustenance that, unfortunately, would render her a black widow yet another time.

The feeling was now at peak strength. It filled her entire body as she moved forward upon her eight black legs. She did not comprehend why but she was one with the monstrous form beneath her.

The others of her kind also communicated hunger. The love feast had come. The timeless ritual. But first there must be mercy and the assurance that the enormous mate would not desert them.

Latrodectus inflicted her bite and saw that the other widows were also injecting their fangs. The enormous mate convulsed several times before slipping into a state of paralysis. At last the living hill beneath them writhed no longer.

As she began to eat, Latrodectus was joyous. She knew that this monstrous mate, unappealing as he might be, would surely be pleased. Surely the males of her kind would be envious. For she was bestowing upon him the ultimate and final act of love.

CHAPTER THIRTEEN

The bog was unearthly that night. The fog that twisted about the colonial mansion assumed foreboding shapes, winding between the chipped wooden pillars and dispersing among the dense vegetation growing alongside the warped walls. The crescent moon was suspended in a beclouded sky. The only other light came from a single first floor window that cut like a yellow eye through the fog and darkness.

Samuel Tate walked from his car, which he had parked beneath a fragrant balsam tree. He removed the .38 Smith & Wesson revolver from the shoulder holster beneath his suit coat. It was the same snub-nose weapon he had carried before the detective agency had retired him. Its weight felt assuring in his hand. And though it had not been used for business since his retirement, it was clean and polished like a black mirror.

Cautiously Tate approached the mansion, his eyes almost hypnotized by the swirling mists. His shoes silently crushed the cranberry and laurel flowers that grew from the soft surface of the bog. He could hear the noises of the many insects, the numbers of which he could not even begin to estimate. That incessant droning should have spurred him to return to his car and drive away. But Samuel Tate moved forward.

He looked about for the Cadillac but did not see the black limousine anywhere. That made him smile; for if the Cadillac weren't there perhaps Grollman wasn't there as well. Tate didn't particularly want to encounter Grollman regardless of his shiny .38.

As Tate walked, he remembered. The executives at the detective agency had said he was no longer fit for the job. The company doctor had examined him and declared that his heart was weak, that he should retire and find some less strenuous profession. That was six years ago. And during those six years Tate had put his knowledge of crime and criminals and his experience in the field to good use, becoming a modestly successful writer of mystery novels. But writing confined him to a desk and a typewriter. And he still craved the excitement and the thrill in deduction that had been his life for eighteen years.

But now he would demonstrate to the agency and to himself that he could still be a good investigator. He had been careful, ever so careful, not to go to the police. He had advised his former fraternity brothers also to remain silent, intimidating them with talk about scandals and law suits. Actually he did not really worry over the possible repercussions of something that happened twenty-five years ago for which the victim probably had no evidence himself. But the involuntarily retired private detective would certainly acquire his own proof against Dr. Reid. Yes, Samuel Tate would prove his worth to everyone.

He stopped suddenly as he saw the door open and a familiar image roll out on the dark porch.

Dr. Ronald Reid, grasping the sides of his wheelchair, moved forward a few inches. His pale face and yellow hair seemed almost white in light of waning moon and gray clouds. There was no expression on his face and his eyes, as before, were hidden behind the bulbous black glasses.

"Hello, Sam," said Dr. Reid in his usual leisurely fashion. "I take it by that gun in your hand, you're not here to have a drink over old times. Well, maybe that's for the better, since my butler isn't around to accommodate you."

He began to roll forward a bit more.

Tate's finger tightened upon the warm trigger of his gun. He raised the revolver in his extended arm, the short barrel aimed directly at the invalid's chest. "Hold it right there," he said. "I may not have had reason to use this for six years. But I've kept up my marksmanship at the target range. And I could easily put a bullet into your chest at the slightest indication that you're up to something."

"Me? Up to something." Dr. Reid laughed. "You're crazy. You must be trying to fabricate a mystery around me, to prove that you still have what it takes to be a detective. Now please, put down that gun."

"Don't kid me, Ronald," said Tate, holding the gun tighter. "Or should I call you by the name that fits you, the name we all called you back then? *Bugs*—"

Dr. Reid gripped the arms of his wheelchair and squirmed in his own confinement. "Then there's no longer any need to lie to you, is there, Sam? It seems as if your old deductive skills aren't burned out afterall. So you've proven that you're still qualified to work in the field. Well, my friend, you'll never be more in the field than you are now."

"I'm going inside the house, Bugs," said Tate, taking a step forward into the squishy ground. "And then I'm going to gather up all the evidence I'll need to put you away somewhere."

"I suppose you have me trapped, Sam. So what can a poor cripple like me do while his strength is out on an errand?"

"Before I go inside, do you want to gloat a bit?" asked Tate.

"Want to tell me how you did it? How you got insects to do what you wanted? To attack men in cars, in their homes?"

"I'm afraid you'll have to wait a little to find that out, Sam," answered Dr. Reid. "But you'll learn soon enough, just as soon as Grollman gets back from Kessler's house. I'll let you guess what he did there. Let me just say that I've tried to make each death appropriate, and that goes for Kessler too. As for you, you'll learn the truth behind my methods soon—first hand."

Tate felt a pang of nausea in his gut. Appropriate, Reid had said. What death could be more appropriate for Kessler than the actualization of his childhood nightmare. And what would be appropriate for him? He looked around but saw no indication that the limousine was returning. There was only the fog and the swamp and the overhead moon. He heard no engine, only the chirping and buzzing of the bog insects.

Smiling, Tate said, "Unless you can control your bugs by mental telepathy, I don't put too much stock in your threats. Because without your flunky here to help you, I doubt there's much you can do from that wheelchair. And I'll be sure to get done with what I'm doing before that lumbering ox returns."

"And nothing I can say will stop you?"

"You've got to be kidding."

Tate was a small man, but the revolver increased his stature over the man in the wheelchair. Poor Kessler, he thought. Kessler had been the last member of their group to die. But perhaps his death would serve a purpose—the purpose of detaining Grollman for a while longer.

He smiled, almost a cruel smile, as he advanced toward the house in long strides. His shoes left impressions in the dead vegetation. His soul seemed to blaze with a new fire, kindled by the sheer helplessness of his wheelchair-ridden opponent.

Dr. Reid's head lowered slightly, as if to watch Tate's feet. He looked up but did not smile as the expression on Tate's face metamorphosed from triumph to shock.

Tate felt the ground vanish beneath his feet and he plunged through blackness. He felt his face torn by jagged branches and his body slammed as it struck the wet ground below. Knees were forced to slam hard into his jaw and Samuel Tate plunged into unconsciousness.

Blackness reigned. And then Tate awakened, his body aching from the impact of the fall. He discovered that he was at the bottom of a deep pit, that reeked with the stench of decayed vegetation. His face stung and when he touched it he found many tiny wounds, all wet and hurting.

From overhead came a mocking laugh. Dr. Reid was at the rim of the pit.

"It's still kind of amusing, Sam," said Dr. Reid, "that you actually believed I'd be out here without some sort of protection. That's actually very funny."

Instead of answering, Tate attempted to climb the walls of his stinking prison. Fingers grasped moist walls. But he was still weak, still in pain and the walls rose up perpendicular, towering at least six or more feet above his head.

Again he heard the jeering laughter. When Dr. Reid was calm, he said in his deep voice, "I reasoned that sooner or later one of you might stumble onto the truth that I was the one responsible. That's why, the morning after the party here, I had Grollman dig this pit and cover it with vegetation. He digs fairly good pits, don't you think? But frankly, Sam, you disappointed me. I thought you'd have come here much sooner than this, say about the time Alex met up with the ants."

Tate again looked about his prison. When he looked back, he saw that Reid had been joined by another man. He was tall, almost a giant, and wearing a worn-out butler's livery. In his hand was a metal spray gun. Grollman smiled sadistically. His upper lip snarled to show sulphur colored teeth.

"What are you going to do to me?" shouted Tate, his voice resounding against the walls of the dark pit.

"Don't tell me your Sherlock Holmes brain hasn't figured that out, Sam," said Dr. Reid. "Let's just say that your friends have all been dying like flies, especially that spineless Kessler whom I managed to turn into a fly so to speak. And so the same is about to happen to you. You probably never heard about pheromones. But do you see that spraygun that Grollman is holding?"

Tate could not miss the formidable looking object that Grollman held like a weapon in one massive hand. From down in the pit, the butler's already large dimensions seemed to take on new and monstrous proportions.

"That spraygun," continued Dr. Reid, moving his hands as though giving a lecture, "contains a chemical compound of my own invention, a synthetic pheromone that can send a predetermined message to a particular species of arthropod. It can arouse in an insect or spider a particular need or craving. I've made all kinds of pheromones, Sam, for all kinds of insects. Each of my pheromones has its own particular message for the insect of my choice.

"You know, Sam, the implications of my discovery are staggering. Other scientists haven't gone as far as I have in pheromone experimentation. Perhaps when I've finished with this business of revenge I'll present my discovery to the scientific community. Perhaps it will benefit mankind. You see, by controlling the instincts of insects, you can accomplish such things as regulating the number of pests. Think of it, Sam! A farmer's crops need not be destroyed by locusts if he could use synthetic pheromones to convince the insects that they aren't hungry.

"But I've also learned to be careful," Dr. Reid went on, "for a misuse of my pheromones could produce tragic results. Take millipedes, for example. Millipedes eat calcium from the earth. But increase their appetites artificially to the point that they eat too much calcium and think of how many other living creatures would eventually be deprived of that necessary element. Luckily, I know what I'm doing, Sam.''

Dr. Reid's voice was unnerving. Tate could feel its effects along his electrified backbone.

''Now all Grollman has to do is release a spray of my synthetic pheromones,'' said the chemist, ''and a horde of insects will emerge from their places in the bog. From under rocks, from beneath vegetation, they'll come. And if you haven't already guessed what feeling is included in the chemical in Grollman's spraygun, if your Sherlock Holmes mind hasn't already figured out that one, I'll say it in one word: *hatred*. What insects will respond? You'll just have to wait and see.''

Tate felt his blood grow cold as he saw the man in the wheelchair nod to the butler. He saw Grollman respond silently, squeezing back the trigger of the spraygun to release a gaseous jet of vapor into the air.

Again gazing down at his captive, Dr. Reid said, ''No need to worry about us, Sam. I've taken precautions with this pheromone. So we can safely watch from up here. You know, I've never actually seen my insects attack one of my hated enemies before. It should prove to be interesting. Wouldn't you say?''

Dr. Reid said no more. There was silence in the bog that existed above the entrapped Samuel Tate. The two men above were listening.

''Damn you, Reid, get me out of here!'' shouted Tate.

But Dr. Reid did not answer. The only response was a distant trilling which was gradually elevating in pitch and volume.

Tate began to sweat. He could feel the liquid pour from his forehead and run down the bony contours of his face. He could taste the salty perspiration trickling into his mouth. His eyes bulged large as he attempted to see what monstrous denizens were marching in response to the chemical spray. So far he could see nothing, only Reid and Grollman, who were both looking down into the pit at their quarry.

At last Dr. Reid said, "Hear them? To a man like me, who's studied insects for over thirty-eight years, those noises are being made by *Tettigonia viridissima,* usually harmless members of the order *Orthoptera*. In nature, these insects eat only vegetation. But with the hatred pheromone Grollman has sprayed into the air, I'm certain they'll turn the powerful mandibles of their masticating mouths on the object of their hatred. Namely, you."

Tettigonia viridissima, Reid had said. To Samuel Tate the name was meaningless. They could be anything and probably were. Their noises were louder, closer, echoing and re-echoing through Tate's ears, his skull, his brain.

Frantically he looked about the pit. His foot inadvertently kicked something hard, something metallic. Stooping he retrieved his fallen revolver. He fired the weapon causing an incandescant flare in the darkness. But the shot was wild, missing the two men at the rim and giving them an opportunity to act. A moment later Grollman had pushed his master out of Tate's line of fire.

Then those who were summoned to hate Samuel Tate appeared at the rim of the pit. There were at least two dozen insects, with long green bodies, with wings pressed against their sleek sides. Harmless grasshoppers, he thought, but when under the control of Ronald Reid—

The first dozen grasshoppers leapt into the pit, latching onto the material of Tate's suit coat and shirt with their strong front legs. Already more of the creatures were lining the rim of the pit. The trilling of the grasshoppers was deafening now. A hundred or more gazed down at him. Now a thousand.

Tate raised his pistol as grasshoppers crawled up his arms and onto his throat. He fired again, bringing explosive light to the darkness. But the bullet that left the smell of gunpowder in the pit vanished into the overhead mists. And Tate realized that this weapon that could have ended Reid's life in an instant was useless against the green horde under his control.

The second squad of grasshoppers jumped into the pit. Hundreds of green, masticating insects bit and chewed this object of their hatred. Tate fired a third time, into the wet wall of the pit, then at the ground beneath his feet where more of the creatures were beginning to spring. He yelled from the grasshoppers biting his hand and dropped the gun. When he managed to look up toward the pit, he saw not only a hundred or more grasshoppers jumping into the fray, but also Grollman wheeling his employer for another look.

"Yes," said Dr. Reid, laughing, "you've still got a lot of the detective in you, Sam. You see how well you've solved the mystery."

As Samuel Tate heard the insane laughter of Ronald Reid and Grollman amid the trilling of the grasshoppers, and as he felt the incessant biting of his flesh by tiny mandibles, he experienced a sharp pang in his chest. Breathing was suddenly impossible. He slumped forward, face smacking against odorous wall. And as his eyes closed upon the hating insects that were leaping upon his face, Tate realized that perhaps the agency doctor's diagnosis was not so wrong after all.

CHAPTER FOURTEEN

Karen was at Gary's apartment Wednesday evening when Richard Kessler phoned. Gary again met her that day following a modeling assignment for a photography magazine. Gary was steadily becoming the main concern in her life. And considering his actions, Karen was the first concern of his. It was good not to be lonely; good to feel love.

She canceled her modeling assignment for Wednesday. The recent deaths of William Bertrand and Alex Gear and the attack on Gary convinced her that she must not leave him for their mutual protection. So, Gary gave her little opposition when she demanded to accompany him out to the bog. She hastily got ready. After a fast brushing of her hair, she called to Gary, "Let's go." He was already halfway out the door.

The white Corvette was presently speeding through the darkness of the bog. Overhanging foliage spilled enormous shadows across the road. The crescent moon peeked through the tops of green-black trees.

Karen watched through the closed window of the sports car,

perceiving the misty vegetation that streaked behind her. Then she turned away from the window; for the swamp only served to rekindle soul-tearing memories. This was her first visit to the swampland since that fateful night of the reunion. She didn't want to see the place where her father had died.

Half expecting another such bombardment by flying insects, Karen looked toward the driver of the Corvette. She observed the strong and angular lines of his rugged face and noted that it was still frozen with grim determination. His eyes were trained upon the windshield. He seemed oblivious to her presence.

"This case means a great deal to you, doesn't it?" asked Karen, providing the first sounds in minutes save for the purr of the automobile and the night noises of the bog.

"A hell of a lot," Gary answered with staid voice. "I don't know how much time we've got left, but there still might be a chance to save Tate."

"Gary," she said, tightening her grip on his knee, "it's not really so much that you want to save Samuel Tate from Dr. Reid, is it? There's something else on your mind. I've been with you long enough to tell."

"I guess it'd be wrong to lie to you, Karen, even at the risk of sounding like an opportunistic pig. First of all, considering how close you and I have become in the short while we've known each other, I must bring your father's murderer to justice."

"That doesn't sound so opportunistic to me. There's more, isn't there?"

"Yeah, there's more. This whole thing could make me, Hon. And I don't want to blow it. This is the first time I've ever been involved in something bigger than a wife beating or a burglary. It's my first chance of doing something really important and making the seven God damn long years I put into this God damn job seem worthwhile. I know I must sound like I'm crazy or something."

Finally Karen smiled. She took his right hand from the steering wheel, bringing it to her lips for a light kiss. Then she brushed his hand against her smooth cheek. That was her reply to Gary.

The Corvette stopped near two other automobiles, one of which was the black Cadillac limousine. Visible through the vapors of the swamp was the mansion of Dr. Ronald Reid with its single luminous first floor window.

The bog was particularly noisesome this night. Every insect stridulation sent a new feeling of apprehension through Karen's nervous system. The powerful stench of decomposing plants attacked her olfactory sense.

Gary gripped two objects in his hands as he and Karen left their car. In one hand he held a flashlight, the beam of which remained off. The other hand held his Colt revolver. "We've got to be careful," he said. "Hope they didn't hear our car pull up."

Things scrambled underfoot as Karen walked close to Gary. She felt something unseen flick against her hand, which prompted her to grasp Gary's steady arm. Instinctively Gary switched on his flashlight, beaming it down at the ground. The yellow light revealed the ten or so ineffectual-looking grasshoppers that were hopping about the vegetation.

Karen didn't smile at the revelation, recalling what apparently harmless insects had done in the past week and a half. She took another step, then suddenly pulled Gary's arm, holding him back. A deep hole in the ground yawned precariously near their feet. Another inch and they would have plunged into jet-black emptiness.

Flashing his beam into the pit, Gary brought the torn corpse to light. Grasshoppers jumped playfully about the lifeless husk. There was enough face left to be recognized as belonging to Samuel Tate.

Nauseous, Karen brought a hand to her mouth, then turned away. The air was cool and a deep draft helped to clear her senses.

"If there was ever any doubt that Reid is the guilty one," said Gary, turning off his beam, "it doesn't exist now. You sure you want to stick this out instead of waiting back in the car?"

Facing him, Karen asked, "Do you really think I'd wait out in this swamp alone, even in a locked car?"

Gary led the way to the mansion. Warily he and Karen peered into the only illuminated window of the house, observing through the filthy glass what appeared to be a laboratory. "That's where we have to go," he said.

The front door to the mansion was locked. Gary aimed his pistol at the lock but then lowered his gun. "What the hell am I doing? I might as well knock on the door and have the butler announce me."

Together they searched for some other means of entrance. Gary thrust his arm through one of the many broken windows, turning the latch and pushing up the window. A minute later Gary and Karen were inside the mansion. The sudden flash of Gary's beam revealed they were in the study. "It's the lab we have to find. And I think I remember its general direction."

They were in the dusty corridor when they heard the faint laughter they recognized as Reid's. The laughter originated beyond a closed door that the detective found to be unlocked. The laughter was louder now. It carried over a cacophony of sounds that Karen recognized as the noises of insects. A cold rush swept Karen as she considered the swarms of insects that might, at any moment, come lashing out through the open door. But as Gary opened the door farther, no insects attacked.

Karen and Gary entered the room. The flashlight showed that it was clean and neat and modern, an anachronism with the rest of the mansion. Tables and shelves lined each wall and supported countless tanks and cages. These containers were alive with noisy insects, so numerous and of so many varieties that Karen could only be overwhelmed by their total effect. She saw mantises, flies, mosquitos, locusts, wasps, dragonflies. *Beetles!* Their stinks filled the room. All of these insects were insane with activity, buzzing about their prisons as if they were attempting to escape.

Other things attracted Karen's attention. Apparently every space not occupied by insects was filled with jars of liquid. The labels she did not understand, but she knew how to collectively describe these liquids. "Pheromones," she said to Gary, seeing him respond with an affirmative nod.

There was also something else in the room. It was metallic and gleamed a silver gray in the meager light of the room—a spraygun only a few feet below what appeared to be a fuse box.

Karen followed Gary as he crept around an L-shaped corner into the following room, and then the next, both of which were filled to capacity with jars and insectariums. At the end of the third room was a half-open door. The laughter was uproarious now, originating from that fourth room. Gary silently opened the door and Karen saw, his back to them—Dr. Ronald Reid.

His laughter was dying now as he sat in his wheelchair in a laboratory cram-full of chemistry equipment. There were racks of test tubes, beakers filled with liquids of varying colors, rubber tubing that connected Bunsen burners to gas jets and heated the liquid contents of test tubes. Glassware reflected the overhead lights. And, as in the other three rooms, there were the expected assortments of captive insects and jars presumably containing yet more pheromones.

The doctor, facing his workbench and its chemistry apparatus, finally ceased to laugh, leaving the insects to create the only noises in the laboratory. Karen looked above his head, noticing the pictures hanging on the wall among the charts and diagrams that depicted the insides of insects. There were six of these unexpected illustrations altogether, all reproductions she recognized as M.C. Escher lithographs and wood engravings.

The first illustration represented two scarabs—beetles—crawling about a circular object. The second showed an enormous preying mantis perched atop the corpse of a bishop. The third was a close-up study of an ant while the fourth depicted nine ants crawling about a Mobius strip. Butterflies interlocking to complete one intricate design constituted the fifth reproduction while the sixth represented a dragonfly on a leaf. The final picture in the series, set way off to the right, showed a fat grasshopper admiring its reflection in a mirrorlike surface.

Dr. Reid finally spoke. "You really ought to drive a less noisy car," he said with supreme confidence. Then he slowly turned his wheelchair to face the young man and woman who stood in the doorway of his laboratory. The Escher illustrations ranged straight line above him. He sat exactly between the two pictures depicting ants. And although his face did not reveal any emotion, his baritone voice sounded as though he were suddenly pleased. "So, I've finally managed to kill off all my enemies. And now look who's here. The police and the daughter of my first victim. I suppose I should be flattered for this unexpected visit."

He was totally insane. Of this Karen had no doubts. She held the flashlight tight in her hand as if it were a weapon.

"I wish I could have stopped you sooner," said Gary stepping forward and raising his revolver to a line parallel with the doctor's pallid face. "But at least I have the satisfaction of knowing that you won't be using pheromones to kill anyone else."

"Pheromones?" There was surprise in Dr. Reid's voice, that

was not reflected on his bearded face. "My, but I didn't know that the police read *Scientific American* or the *Annual Review of Entomology*. Did you learn that at the academy, Sergeant?"

"You can shove the sarcasm, Reid," said Gary. "You see, I'm going to wheel you out of this tomb and take you where you won't be able to do any more harm. And you know, I think this city will be looking on Sgt. Gary Rutledge in a new light once the newspapers get the whole story."

"So you'll play the hero right to the end, Sergeant?"

Karen cringed at the way Dr. Reid had pronounced *end*. But she was more concerned with someone other than Reid—that monster in a butler's uniform who towered nearly seven feet tall. So far Grollman had not made an appearance. But Reid's arrogance made her believe that the giant was lurking somewhere within the shadows of the mansion.

Still holding the gun, Gary walked to the rear of the wheelchair and started pushing it toward the door.

"Be careful, Gary," said Karen. "Remember Grollman."

"Yes indeed," mocked the chemist. "Above all, don't forget Grollman."

"I remember," said Gary in monotone. "And I'm watching for him."

It was not until Gary had wheeled the doctor out of the laboratory and turned the corner into the corridor that the giant struck. Grollman had apparently slipped into the room unheard while the detective was with Reid. The butler, his black uniform serving as camouflage, sprang from obsidian shadows. He was incredibily fast for one of such bulk. Iron fingers gripped the back of Gary's neck, yanking him away from the wheelchair. An animalistic snarl hissed from Grollman's throat as the giant effortlessly tossed his captive out of the room and into the adjacent hallway.

"That's it, Grollman," said Dr. Reid with concern. "Keep

him out there and get rid of his gun."

Karen saw Gary get to his feet.

Angry and still clutching his pistol, he raised it for a shot. But Grollman was upon him before he could squeeze the trigger, grabbing his arm so that the inevitable explosion of gunfire sent its projectile harmlessly down the length of the corridor.

Teeth clenched, Grollman squeezed Gary's arm tighter. The detective's hand lost its color and the gun dropped uselessly to the discolored rug. A look of anguish appeared on Gary's face as the snarling butler closed his vise fingers tighter still.

"Gary!" exclaimed Karen. She started to run toward the corridor. Perhaps there was something she could do for Gary. But as she moved Dr. Reid also moved, seizing her wrist in his pincerlike grip, forcing her to drop the flashlight. Karen felt not only fear as he clutched her flesh, but also revulsion. His touch was cold, and wet. His body shook spasmodically as he began to laugh. And still that expressionless face hardly moved.

Again she looked toward Gary. He struggled to break the giant's hold. By the expression on his face she could imagine the strength in Grollman's enormous hand. Then the butler formed a massive fist with his free hand. With almost crushing impact he slammed it into Gary's jaw.

Blood splattered from Gary's face. Eyes wide, blazing with cruel rage, Grollman struck him again. Gary's head wobbled senselessly, his neck still confined in the giant's grip. More blood spilled from his mouth. A third blow to his skull sent him sprawling against the wall and dropping limply to the floor.

Karen was still struggling against Reid's slimy grip. There were noises of insects, presumably trying to burst from their cages and tanks, as Karen commanded all her strength and finally pulled herself free. Then with no concern other than Gary, she bolted into the corridor. Hurrying to his apparently lifeless body, she stooped, knelt, coddled his unknowing head, touched the scarlet stream that leaked from his wounds. "Gary . . . Gary . . ."

He did not respond, not even with as much as a groan. The only answer to her voice rumbled from above. "He ain't gonna hear you for a long time, girlie."

Karen gazed up at the hulking creature. Now that she was on her knees Grollman seemed twice as tall as before. He stood confident with his boulder fists spreading fingers and lowering toward her. A licentious grin split his apish face. Bushy eyebrows lifted while eyes moved in their sockets to caress the woman's body with their gaze.

Snapping her head to one side, she looked down the corridor. She knew that it extended to the vestibule and then the front door. For a moment Gary, alive or dead, was erased from her thoughts. She existed, Grollman existed. She had to escape from him before those mammoth hands touched her. In one surge of energy Karen sprang to her feet. With long strides she dashed down the darkened corridor and made it to the vestibule.

"Stop her, Grollman!" she heard Reid exclaim behind her.

The lights flashed on as she rushed towards the front door, her only barrier to freedom. The door was locked from the inside. Her fingers frantically struggled with the complicated mechanism of the old fashioned lock. But even as she began to unlock the door, she could hear ponderous footsteps getting louder behind her.

She did not turn to look until two herculean hands gripped her from behind. The right hand pressed hard against her flat stomach while the other crawled over her right breast. Struggling, she could not break Grollman's steel embrace. With a quick jerk of her head, Karen sank her teeth into the giant left hand, biting hard until the fingers finally relaxed, accompanied by a raspy snarl of pain. She was momentarily free but the door was still locked.

Grollman steamed with rage. "You're gonna pay for that, you little bitch!" he roared as he grabbed her shirt and ripped it. "And only one of us is gonna be happy."

Karen could not determine whether the hideous expression on Grollman's face was made of hatred or desire. His nostrils flared like two bottomless black pits. Then he raised the hand that still bore the impressions of her teeth and slapped the side of her head with just enough force to send her reeling and keep her conscious. She hit the door, then dropped. And through blurry eyes she could see the scowling butler breathing heavily, hands descending for her.

"You don't know how I wanted to do this ever since that night in the bog when I first saw you," he said, gasping. Now there was a bizarre tenderness in his voice that Karen had not deemed possible. That tenderness only served to make his words the more ominous. "The way you looked in that skimpy blue dress," he went on, his large and sweating face moving closer to her. "The way your yellow hair blew in the wind. The way . . ."

He dropped to his knees with a loud thud and gaped at Karen like an adolescent mooning over his first love. There was a tragic innocence about his twisted face. Yet in that innocence was a wild-eyed leer that made Karen writhe even before he touched her with his fingers.

Gently the butler brushed along the lines of her legs, then paused over the tanned bare skin of her hips and waist. Karen hit him hard. But Grollman reacted. His eyes inflamed with desire. Then, as she pressed against the door, he reached out for her.

"Grollman!" The voice from the far end of the corridor was commanding, resonant with authority. "What's taking you so long? Bring the Barks girl back here!"

"Shit!" moaned Grollman. Then he grabbed one of the girl's shivering arms and slapped her again.

Karen's head spun from the blow. She felt the floor vanish as Grollman bore her up in his burly arms. She was weak but knew that even Gary could not break that almost superhuman grip. There was a hazy image of a bleeding Gary lying in a heap upon the floor.

A minute later she was dropped roughly into a chair. She managed a hazy glimpse of Reid, rolling toward her in his wheelchair, and speaking to the giant butler who still held the girl's arms so that she could not move.

"Tie her up," ordered Dr. Reid. "And then get rid of that detective's corpse."

Grollman began to obey the doctor's command as the insects in the room boomed and chirped and seemed to beg for release.

CHAPTER FIFTEEN

The coarse ropes that secured Karen to the old creaking chair were tight. Their rough broken fibers pressed uncomfortably into her skin. She struggled to break her bonds, but Grollman must have been a sailor once for his dexterity with knots. Then she stopped her futile attempts. For what could she do against Grollman and Reid even if she did manage to free herself?

Grollman was still staring at her. The yellow teeth in his gaping mouth seemed more yellow in the laboratory lights. His eyes were still trained upon her ripped shirt and the exposed flesh beneath.

"Quit gawking at her," said Dr. Reid. "And get rid of the corpse that's littering my corridor."

Grollman acted efficiently. He stomped out of the laboratory, looking back only once at Karen. Moments later the sounds of footsteps and something being dragged faded down the hallway. Then there sounded the unlocking and opening of the front door.

Dr. Reid moved his wheelchair close to Karen. "Grollman is

really quite obedient, he does whatever I tell him. That's because I pay him well and sometimes let him have his fun with the experimental insects. He also knows that if he does what I tell him to do, someday, after I've presented my discovery to the world where it will hopefully benefit humanity, he'll share in the profits and glory. I think he likes his expected rewards even better than he likes you, Karen."

The chemist rolled within a few inches of Karen's face. This was the closest she had ever been to him. His eyes were still hidden behind the dark semi-globes that were his glasses. The blond mustache, beard and hair were perfectly groomed.

When next he spoke, Dr. Reid raised his voice to carry over the chirruping and booming of his experimental insects. "You know," he said, "I've done what other scientists have only begun to play with—the control of insects by man. And I've put that discovery to good use. For while the more orthodox men of science were fooling with moth pheromones, I actually accomplished something, went beyond them all. I've used my advanced discoveries in pheromones to eliminate my enemies in the most fitting ways I could devise. Only now can I relax and use my synthetic pheromones for the altruistic reasons they were originally created."

Karen felt her tears coming. She had first lost her father to this madman. And now the only other man she had ever grown to love was dead and dragged off somewhere by Grollman, no doubt to feed more of Reid's insect slaves. But even though she grieved, she could not escape the curiosity welling up within her. "But why," she blurted out, staring directly into the chemist's dark lenses. "What did my father . . . what did those others . . . ever do to you to make you do this?"

Grollman entered the laboratory and stood menacingly in the doorway before Dr. Reid could answer. "I got rid of the body," said the butler gruffly, "just like you wanted." He was looking at Karen again with expectation written on his face, making her feel sick.

Stroking his yellow beard, Dr. Reid finally replied. "I suppose every genius wants to share his successes with someone. Obviously, when I do present my discoveries to the scientific community, I will have to delete certain details. I won't be able to tell them about my practical experiments. And obviously, Grollman knows what I've done and why I've done it. But Grollman couldn't care less. So you should feel honored, Karen, because you'll be the first and only person to ever know the whole truth."

Then wheeling himself about the laboratory and gesturing theatrically with his hands, Dr. Ronald Reid slowly dramatized his narrative to the background music of thousands of tiny creatures:

I had been interested in arthropods, especially insects, since I was a child. Actually this was more than an interest or a hobby. It was really a scientific study that I made on my own while other children were out playing baseball in the street. Most of my free time was spent indoors, reading books about insects. Insects fascinated me. There was something compelling about the fact that they existed upon this planet for so many thousands of millenia.

Weekends usually found me at the Marshall Natural History Museum. They had an impressive entomology exhibition hall on the first floor. I'd spend hours looking with wonder upon the beautiful little creatures pinned down and preserved behind their cases of glass. So inspired was I that I eventually began to go into the forest on field trips with my father and collect insects of my own. Soon I possessed a rather impressive collection of insects pinned to old shirt boxes. When merely collecting began to bore me, and my insects were stored away in closets, I found new satisfaction in raising live insects in my father's basement.

When I entered high school, the adolescent students derided me for my ever growing interest in entomology. My social life was one depressing zero and only then did I realize just what I had missed throughout my elementary school years. But though I was a washout in enjoying the company of others, I was a self-taught expert in entomology. Voraciously, I devoured every scrap of information that was available to me on insects. Yes, I was a damned authority at seventeen.

Yet, by the time I entered my senior year at high school, I began to yearn for the social life I had inadvertently deprived myself of. Girls shunned me, calling me that "crazy bug-boy." Once, I fumbled with the words that would hopefully get me a date for the senior prom with a rather plain-looking girl. I met her in chemistry class and it was at the end of the period that I worked up the nerve to ask her. She refused me bluntly, loud enough for the other students to hear, saying that she wouldn't be touched by someone whose fingers had only fondled maggots and roaches all his life. That required many sleepless nights to overcome.

When I entered college the same year that my father died, I hoped to change all that and begin a whole new life. The science scholarship I had won afforded me the means to work at a degree in entomology. But I swore to make an effort to fulfill the social needs of my life. In those days social life was virtually synonymous with fraternities and sororities.

During my second freshman semester I became quite a close friend of William Bertrand, a student in my biology class. Willie did his best to convince me to pledge the fraternity he had joined the semester before. To someone like me who had gone friendless through most of his years, such an offer was impossible to turn down. So I went down to the cafeteria where the fraternity had their own table. There I met the brothers. The brothers that joined the same time as Willie seemed to take an immediate liking to me. There was Dick Kessler, who had little ambition other than getting through school. Alex Gear, whose greatest love after the fraternity itself was the school ROTC, in which he was a lieutenant. And Bryant Krass, who spent more time at Kelly's than he did in classes and the cafeteria combined. And Harvey Lance, who seemed to take special delight in the comraderie of the organization. Let's not forget Sam Tate, whose greatest pleasure seemed to be reading Sherlock Holmes and Ellery Queen stories. Of course, we mustn't overlook your father and the way he relentlessly snapped pictures at every school and fraternity function; a real camera bug.

They came on all smiles and warmth. Pledge their fraternity, they said, and I'd be among the campus elite. I told them of my interest in entomology and that I intended to specialize in that field. It didn't seem to matter with them. They accepted me, insects and all. Or so I thought.

At first I tried not to blame them for what happened once pledging opened for that semester. I thought they were really my friends and that their hazing was just part of the fraternity "game." But they remembered too well their own hazing from the semester before and were more than eager to take out their corked revenge on someone. Since my seeming obsession with entomology made me appear different from the other six pledges, I was the target for every sadistic trick they could devise.

To begin, they nicknamed me "Bugs." The damned name spread quickly about the school to the extent that even people not associated with the fraternity called me that. After a while the name gnawed at my nerves. And every time someone called me that I felt a part of me die.

Certainly there were the usual pledge chores that every pledge had to perform; calling the brothers "Mister" and "Sir," waiting on the brothers at the table, that sort of thing. But every time I served them their food from the counter, I received some castigation about my filthy insect-touching claws contaminating their food. At parties, when I was technically not pledging, I was still the butt of their jokes. Girls at parties made fun of me along with the brothers until "Bugs" Reid was a mere buffoon for everyone with a sadistic urge to take a stab at.

Still, so starved was I for friendship of any kind, that I endured it all, believing that when pledging was over and after I went through initiation, I'd be just another one of the group. Then I could have a social life and continue my entomological studies.

But then came initiation night—"Hell Night," they so rightly called it. I swear my initiation was more severe than that of any of the other six pledges. Blindfolded, I walked into the room of the cheap hotel where they held that semester's initiation. Some of the brothers dumped crackers or something over me while Tate—I'll never forget his voice, the skinny little bastard—yelled that they were grasshoppers hopping all about their "Royal Majesty, King Bugs the First."

Somehow I managed to endure the initiation. Now I was a full-fledged brother in the fraternity. There was a semi-formal dinner at which I received my pin. But when Howard bestowed my pin upon me in front of all the acting members of the fraternity, he called me "Bugs" and the entire assemblage erupted with laughter. Damn him!

The weeks that followed were more hell than "Hell Night" could ever have been. For although I was technically a brother, I was castigated like a pledge. Not a day passed that someone, either a fraternity member or not, did not deride me in some way involving insects. I've forgotten how many caterpillars or dead bees were slipped onto my plate in the cafeteria. Someone—to this day, I don't know who—managed to drop a living fly into my bowl of soup; and when I asked what it was doing there, all six of those bastards yelled simultaneously, "The backstroke!"

What could I do? I wanted so much to be accepted by this group that I'd spent nearly a full semester pledging. A drastic move was in order. I changed my major to chemistry in the hopes of making a good impression on everyone.

My second year at college, I was an ardent chemistry student. But my change in majors did not diminish the cruelties heaped upon me by my supposed friends. Eventually I was pressured into transferring to another college on the pretext that it offered a better chemistry program. Still the brothers would not let me alone. They resented my "deserting" them, they said, for I had become a part of their lives, the focus of their sadistic impulses. And so they continued with their little pranks, forcing themselves to be more creative than they had ever been. They mailed me parcels of living ants. They smashed boxes of termites on my porch. Then one evening while I was at my new university attending a science symposium that lasted all day and evening, during which I listed to a lecture concerning theories of communication between arthropods, a group of brothers—or perhaps only one brother; I'll never know for sure—dealt me their most insidious blow.

Somehow they broke into my house. Perhaps Tate performed the actual break-in, since he was obsessed with mystery stories and could have learned from them how to tamper with locks. Totally unsuspecting that my loyal brothers had paid me a clandestine visit, I entered the house bubbling with new ideas concerning insect communication. I casually removed my coat and opened the closet door. But I found not only my wardrobe, but a rather unwelcome surprise. Damn them! When I think of what they did, it infuriates me as much today as it did when it happened.

What sheer sadistic cunning! The bastards had placed a hornet's nest in my closet. Believe me, those insects resented their confinement in the closet—which could have included all day and evening. And since I was the one who opened that door, the hornets regarded me as the one responsible for their confinement. They attacked me in droves, going for my face until it was an agonizing pool of blood. Have you ever been stung by a hornet? Well, multiply the pain by the hundreds and you might begin to understand my reactions that followed. Screaming like a baby, I ran outside, dashing blindly into the poorly lit street . . . oblivious to the panel truck that was speeding toward me . . .

After recovering from the accident in the hospital, I disappeared as far as the fraternity brothers were concerned. I used my inheritance to buy this old mansion. It was located in a secluded area of the bog where I could resume my studies and experiments in entomology and chemistry without interruption. There were millions of insects in this peaceful refuge. Here I could study them in an environment still unravaged by man. This was an area in which I could work in complete privacy.

I sent each of the six fraternity brothers a letter saying that I bore no grudge against him and that we should all erase from our minds everything that had happened between us. I was careful not to mention the incident with the hornets, pretending it never occurred. I doubted any of them had the nerve to return to the house to see the results of their little joke. I concluded the letter with the mention that I'd moved to another state, again under the pretext of finding a university with a better chemistry department. The name of the state remained my secret—though I really never left. Finally I added a P.S. that someday we might all get together again.

For over twenty-five years I worked out my revenge. A good stroke of luck happened my way shortly after I moved into this old house and set up my laboratory. Grollman's car broke down nearby. He hated insects, loved money and had no feelings whatsoever about humanity in general. And so he accepted the job I offered him. Grollman served as butler, chauffeur and laboratory assistant. He was with me in the ensuing years while I continued to learn . . . to experiment . . . to combine my knowledge of entomology and chemistry to use in plotting a most stunning vengeance.

I experimented for a long while with pheromones. And since you and your policeman friend seem to already know about these chemical compounds, I won't bore you with the details. Suffice it to say that my synthetic pheromones permitted me to manipulate vast hordes of insects to kill off every one of my enemies. Whenever possible each death, I decided, would befit the victim. My use of bed bugs gave me particular satisfaction. It was the frosting on an already delicious cake. Oftentimes, I was forced to import certain species of insects for the strongest effect, like the swallowtail I knew would lure that fop Harvey Lance to his death. Grollman always made the deliveries while the victims weren't home.

Precautions had to be taken so that my insects would attack only my enemies. I'm not a fiend, Karen. And I had no desire to harm anyone other than those six members of the fraternity. Therefore, unlike the vast majority of the pheromones you see in the jars within this laboratory, the ones Grollman sprayed in the vicinity of my victim's homes were special. To completely work they required a second chemical which I sprayed over the invitations that I mailed out for the reunion. The chemical was activated by a human being's body temperature. Whosoever removed the treated invitation from its protective envelope got the chemical into his pores. The effect was extremely long-lasting. If the invitation happened to be touched when the chemical was still freshly active, no amount of washing could remove it. And it required many days to wear off. Perhaps now you'll understand why you weren't touched when I sent my beetles after your father.

Now Karen, I hope you understand my motives.

Unconsciously, Karen struggled with her bonds, momentarily forgetting the futility of such an attempt.

Dr. Reid was moving still closer. His hand reached his dark glasses, removed them, exposing the bluest eyes she had ever seen—eyes burning with mad fire. Breathing heavily, he leered into Karen's face and she could see the strange lines, resembling circles of cut rubber, that enclosed each eye. She detected a familiar odor, the smell of cosmetics.

"And now do you want to see what no one other than myself and Grollman has seen?" he roared with slow force. "Do you want to know why I've been a cripple, confined to this wheelchair like the insects in this laboratory are confined to their insectariums? Want to see the results of that college prank and the accident that followed? Well, then—"

Karen's heart pounded fiercely. Her eyes were focused upon the doctor's hands as they clutched at the khaki blanket that covered his legs. The hands tore the blanket aside, and revealed a pair of artificial legs.

"So you see, don't you?" roared Dr. Reid, unfastening the wooden legs and hurling them contemptuously against the floor to leave stumps that ended at mid-thigh. "The accident left me only half a man. But, you might ask, would such a handicap, suffered by many people on this Earth, cause a man to commit murder? Well, you've only seen one result of the prank—that left me not only half a man, but also half monster!"

Then in one sweeping movement, Dr. Reid grasped the back of his head and yanked away the realistic mask and blond hair that concealed the horror beneath. The saddle-brown flesh, now dried and withered like the hide of a mummy, barely covered the jagged skull underneath. The lips were virtually nonexistant. The nose was a mere peg, ending abrupt and jagged. The hair was the appearance of light brown straw, hanging wildly about the skull-head. And from the blackened sockets of this leering Grim Reaper seered two insane and hating blue orbs.

"Do you know what it's like, Karen," he said, thrusting back his hideous visage and laughing madly, "can you even begin to comprehend that you've not only been made a cripple, but you've also been transformed into a mockery of the Phantom of the Opera?" His laughter was of such force that his legless torso shimmied violently in the wheelchair.

Karen gasped. She wanted to turn away. But while Reid's deathlike face horrified her, it also fascinated her.

She saw him wheel himself toward one of the workbenches. He was scanning the labels on the pheromone jars as he spoke again.

"And so I've finally been able to tell somebody what I've done," he said. "They say that confession is good for cleansing a guilty conscience, and I must admit this session has had its therapeutic value even though I feel justified in what I've done. But as you've probably guessed by now, the knowledge you've just received is a deadly thing. Therefore, since I've satisfied my need to boast or confess, depending on your disposition, I've got to use my pheromones one more time tonight."

"What do you mean?" she said, knowing the answer she would receive.

"Let's just say," he went on, removing one of the jars from its shelf, "that, although I didn't plan to take any more lives with my chemicals, now I've got no choice. I suppose I can rationalize it, tell myself that this will only make my revenge that much sweeter since you are, after all, a part of Howard Barks. At any rate, Karen, these pheromones will act directly. You won't need any gimmick, like chemically-treated invitations, to make them work."

For a last time she tried to break the bonds but succeeded only in receiving a rope burn about her wrists. She saw Dr. Reid bring the jar before his ghastly countenance and silently read the label. Again there sounded his maniacal howling.

When his laughter finally subsided Reid stated, "I suppose your death should remain consistent with the other deaths. It should have some kind of significance. That's why I've selected a very special species of insect for you, a species that I breed in several of my insectariums here in the laboratory. It will also be in keeping with the insects that devoured your father in the bog."

He turned the jar so that Karen could read the label. The words made her jerk within the confines of her ropes.

"Dermestid beetles!" she said, her eyes staring incredulously at the label on the jar.

"My, I'm impressed!" said Dr. Reid with ridiculing laughter. You seem to be familiar with dermestids. And judging by that look on your pretty face, I'd suspect you know what they're capable of doing."

Grollman, still watching like a silent sentry, groaned.

"Oh, I'm sorry, Grollman," said Dr. Reid. "Of course, before the dermestids finish off our witness, you can have your fun."

Karen's face paled as she saw the giant butler. He was anxiously stalking toward her, desire scrawled upon his sweaty face. His fingers spread to claim her. Giant hands clamped about her shoulders, slowly ripping away her white and red shirt, while Dr. Reid, still holding the jar, resumed his chilling chortling.

CHAPTER SIXTEEN

Darkness spread around him. Darkness and a pungent stench like that which pervaded the laboratory. The smell of insects. There was also a sound, a quiet trilling. And the cold.

Hands moved and touched dampness, felt soggy matter squish between fingers. Head ached as though the skull were nearly split. Taste of blood in his mouth; drying blood. Hair hung against closed eyes. He began to move, crawl, encounter an object wet and lifeless.

Gary Rutledge opened his eyes to see a blur of twisting colors and shapes pulsating in a black void. Vision was painfully returning and he now was cognizant of his whereabouts. He was at the bottom of a dank pit. Struggling to stand, his aching head swirling, he could see the half gnawed corpse of Samuel Tate which was still a haven for clusters of grasshoppers. Several of the insects leaped from the torn carcass and onto Gary's hands. He might have crushed the tiny killers had not his skull been wracked by pain. To his surprise, the grasshoppers appeared to be their normal playful selves, behaving as he had always seen them before anyone began talking about pheromones.

The pit seemed to be about twelve feet deep. Gary wondered if the impact of striking the bottom had served to revive him, or if it were the chirring of the grasshoppers or the feel of their legs against his body. But he wanted to believe that he was simply too tough a cop to let a few blows to the head, even those dealt by a giant like Grollman, keep him unconscious for long.

An image materialized in his mind, a blonde image he had momentarily forgotten while regaining his senses. *Karen!* Was it already too late to save her? He did not know how long he had lain in the pit. Perhaps it was not so long that she was already a victim of Dr. Reid.

With a shake of his head, Gary sent his dirty hair flying out of his face. He saw that the walls of the pit were steep. But standing atop Tate's chest lessened the distance to the opening. Hands digging into facing pit wall, fingers gripping hard the damp substance, muscles straining and bulging, he began to pull himself upward. Gary's head spun; the toes of his shoes kicked into the walls. With considerable effort he was slowly making his way to the rim. Repeating the process of digging and kicking and pulling himself upward, Gary finally reached his destination. Head emerged; he breathed fresh air, then staggered to his feet on the soft ground.

He moved close to the mansion and peered in through the laboratory window. Dr. Reid's back was to him. But he could read the terror on Karen's face as the brute Grollman proceeded to tear at her shirt. He saw her squirm as the butler rubbed his hands across her flesh.

Gary's blood raced. Unspoken curses were uttered in the silent depths of his soul. Moving fast, he discovered that the front door of the mansion was open a crack. Soon he was silently sprinting through the dust beclouded rooms, finally entering the first of the anterooms that preceeded Dr. Reid's laboratory and was hidden around the L-corner. He could hear Karen's moaning, hear Grollman's apish grunts of pleasure, hear the doctor's portentious cackling to the accompaniment of lively insects.

Furtively Gary's eyes darted about the darkened room, perceiving the place as a whole, taking in the jars, the insectariums, the spraygun, the fuse box on the wall. His movements were by rote, as if he'd done this a dozen times before. First he opened the metal tank beneath the spraygun. Next he reached for one of the jars of pheromones, reading in the light from the hallway the label with its meaningless words: *Leptoconops irritans*. He twisted off the lid and, being extremely careful not to let the liquid touch his skin, poured the synthetic pheromone into the spraygun tank. When the spraygun was again ready for use, Gary turned to the fuse box. He could hear Grollman grunting with delight from the farthest room around the corner. Vengefully the detective pulled the fuses from their sockets.

The light that sent a pale nimbus around the L-corner went black.

"Shit!" came the butler's gruff voice from the direction of the laboratory. "What happened to the lights?"

"It must be a blown fuse," said the voice of Dr. Reid. "Take care of it."

Gary heard heavy footsteps approach from the laboratory. Holding the weighty spraygun, he took concealment against the wall by the door connecting with the next anteroom. Grollman was cursing as he lumbered into the room. His goliath frame was a foreboding silhouette in the dim light from the corridor as he proceeded to the fuse box and began to fumble with its insides. "Huh?" he snorted with confusion. "There ain't any fuses in their God damn sockets."

"There 'ain't' any," Gary softly mocked from the shadows, careful so his voice would not carry above the insects' chirping and back to the laboratory, "because I yanked them out."

Gary saw the shadowed look of hatred that boiled on Grollman's brutish face. The butler's sloping brow wrinkled with additional lines. His cold eyes narrowed from beneath the heavy black and gray eyebrows. "You!" he snarled through clenched teeth. "You son of a bitch! I thought I killed you!"

"Confident ape, aren't you, Grollman!"

"Shut up! This time I'm finishing you off for good."

His hand dipped inside his uniform and produced a familiar weapon—Gary's own revolver.

Gary took a step forward. He raised the spraygun, feeling the liquid contents splashing within the tank. The metal reflected the light from the corridor into the giant's face, causing him to react, first with surprise and then with a snide grin.

"What do you think you can do with an empty spraygun?" he growled. "Especially when I got this!" He lifted the pistol, aimed it at Gary's skull.

Gary squeezed back the trigger of the spraygun. A stream of vapor issued from the device, engulfing Grollman in a cloud of synthetic pheromone.

Grollman snarled but did not fire. He writhed, lashing about at the drifting mists with flailing hands. A gutteral cough bellowed from his throat. A sudden expression of horror, the only such look that Gary had ever seen on the butler's face, contorted his features. Then, eyes blinking, Grollman took a step forward and again raised his gun.

Another stream spewed from the spraygun, again enveloping Grollman, again stopping him before he could advance another step or use the revolver. Gary stepped back, careful not to encounter any of the stream, holding back the trigger until the spraygun was empty.

The reaction on Grollman's face was both of terror and anger. He paused, listening to a distant buzzing sound that seemed to originate from somewhere outside the building. His enormous frame was shaking slightly as he gaped about, looking out toward the corridor. Then he turned, again facing Gary.

"You damn fool!" shouted Grollman through his teeth, almost crying. "For what you just did, I'm gonna kill you real special!"

But Gary's movements were almost blinding. With a surge of all of his strength, he raised the empty spraygun over his head, then hurled it hard into Grollman's face.

Grollman reeled as the spraygun bounced off his hard skull and smashed into a shelf of pheromones, splashing wet shards of glass about the floor and over the butler's body. The giant moaned, dropping the revolver, his momentum hurling him crashing into more of the glass jars and bathing him in more of Dr. Reid's pheromones. His mammoth body thudded against the work bench, knocking over an insectarium of wasps that smashed against the floor, releasing its collection of hovering life.

The buzzing sound that emanated from outside was louder now. Grollman turned again toward the corridor to behold an approaching black cloud that paled even his twisted face. "No! Not them!" he barked, transfixed as they encircled his head. "N-not flies. *F-filthy flies*!"

Revulsion seized Gary as he saw the giant butler suddenly revert to a helpless infant. He whimpered as the flies buzzed about his head, oblivious to the fact that his strength was equal to that of several men. But Grollman's strength was meaningless. The butler could only wave his arms in a last effort to fend off the buzzing swarm—and bellow with fear.

Grollman shrieked as his head was enveloped by the hunger-crazed flies. He screamed until his scream became a choke, drowned by the hundred biting flies—flies that might prefer excrement to human flesh—congregating in his gaping mouth.

Like some spasmodic puppet, Grollman went berserk, thrashing his long arms wildly, but succeeding only in smashing more jars of pheromones and more cages and tanks of insects.

Gary turned away from the pitiful Grollman as the hovering wasps also joined in the fray and as another stream of flies buzzed into the room. He looked toward the gun-metal black object on the floor. If he could reach it— But no, the weapon was in the midst of the conflict, with at least fifteen praying mantises walking over and around it.

Gary heard the activity of the swamp. More insects, aroused by the pheromones, he thought, on the march or in flight to join in the feast. He brought his hand to his mouth, fought an urge to vomit. He heard Dr. Reid call out from the darkness of the laboratory, "Grollman, what's going on back there?"

But Grollman didn't answer. He could only lunge about without any purpose than to shake off the hungry and hating insects that were pouring in from the corridor and streaming out of the miniature prisons he inadvertently continued to break. Then, pulling down still more jars, Grollman sank to the floor, where more of his attackers waited expectantly.

As he turned to enter the second anteroom, Gary's foot struck something. It was the flashlight that Karen must have dropped while Grollman was beating him to senseless pulp.

And outside Grillus did not understand. There was something different about the Call this night. Were there many Calls? Why did he feel as if many forces were guiding him?

Grillus hungered. He hated. Loved. Still other emotions sizzled within him, all of which had not been there only a short while before. All of which moved him simultaneously.

He crept from beneath the giant jungle. His antennae undulated, first at the crescent moon suspended in a hazy overhead sea. But the moon, that deity who periodically swelled and slimmed, was suddenly without significance. All that had meaning was Grillus and his minions and the queer distortions of the Call—distortions that were changing Grillus, allowing him, for the first time, to see as he had never seen before.

Awareness was coming. Instinct within instinct. Beyond instinct. Confused awareness.

Grillus turned his head toward the massive angular structure from which the demon fires blazed. From there the Call issued and swept with the evening breeze. This was the place that controlled him, compelled him to hate when he should not hate, hunger for flesh when he truthfully hungered for jungle. Awakening; not from the sleep of inactivity, but from ignorance. This was where he and his kind must go.

Grillus' antennae wavered again amid the drifting messages of the Call. They continued to move until his own message mingled with that of the Call to summon his brothers from the shadows of the bog.

The others responded, assembling before him as a powerful nation. And they all felt the domination of the Call and the need for satisfaction. Following their leader Grillus, the crickets flowed toward the structure, converging upon the points from which the Call originated. There was food in their midst. Writhing, thrashing food. Sustenance that was already feeding other beings similar to themselves. Beings that hummed and buzzed and flew and crawled.

Awareness told Grillus that the origins of his dilemmas existed within dark proximity. Now that the Call had awakened him, he would act with motivations. But for the moment, there were feelings to fulfill. And as he began to fill himself, Grillus looked toward the opening in the chamber where the meager light shone—seeing other inhabitants of his world who were also marching and flying toward the feast.

As Gary heard the disturbing noises that sounded behind him, he turned his flashlight into the laboratory. The beam showed

Karen's disheveled form. She was bound to the chair, her long hair falling over her torn clothing. She called "Gary!" But Karen's pleading visage seemed to vanish in the presence of the cackling thing that also sat revealed in the beam of Gary's flashlight.

The creature had no legs and its face resembled a living death's head. Mad blue eyes blazed from dark tunnels and made a hideous contrast against the taut brownish hide. In one of the creature's hands was a glass tank of insects, their booming sounds striking a discordant note of remembrance in Gary's mind. The other hand clutched a jar of pheromone. And when the creature spoke, rolling forward several inches in its wheelchair, it was in the Dr. Ronald Reid's baritone voice.

"I thought Grollman was efficient," said Dr. Reid. He set the insectarium in his lap and began to unscrew the lid of the jar. "But apparently he didn't do such a terrific job of killing you after all. Judging from those violent noises I just heard from the anterooms, and from the fact that you're standing here alone, I'd guess that you somehow killed him instead. No matter, really," he continued, dropping the lid to the floor. "I don't really need him anymore, because I've killed off all my enemies. And there's enough chemical compound in this jar for both you and Karen to feed my dermestid beetles."

"Be careful, Gary," warned Karen.

But Gary did not look at her. His attention was riveted to the opened jar in the chemist's hand. Its fluid contents reflected the beam of his flashlight. He heard sounds from behind that, Dr. Reid, judging from his unabashed confidence, must have believed were merely his own captive insects reacting with increased vehemence. In another moment Dr. Reid would splash his deadly creation and then release the dermestids from their cage. Then Gary and the woman he loved would suffer the same end as the rhinoceros iguana he'd seen being devoured at the museum.

Reid raised the sloshing liquid slightly above his head. The skull head turned toward Karen, its teeth clenched in a perpetual grin. "Since Karen is related to Howard Barks, I'll give her the honor of dying first."

Karen quivered beneath her ropes. Her brown eyes watched the movement of Dr. Reid's hand as it began to vibrate, as it prepared to throw.

Yet before Dr. Reid could fling his diabolic weapon, the brownish skull turned toward the door behind Gary. There was a sound of feet shuffling toward the laboratory.

"Well," said Dr. Reid, "it appears you're not such an efficient killer either." Then raising his voice, he commanded, "Grollman, get in here. You can hurt the sergeant a little before I turn him into beetle food."

The sound was louder now, just outside the doorway. Gary cautiously stepped away from the door and Dr. Reid continued to look in that direction. The detective could perceive the tall figure of a man in the doorway, silhouetted by the light of the moon from the window. He moved with apparent effort, more like a robot than a man, and stopped in front of Reid.

"Grollman?" said Dr. Ronald Reid.

The figure that could only be Grollman reeked of insects and blood. The figure did not speak. But then, unexpectedly, it began to buzz and chip and boom, hum and chirr.

Gary raised his flashlight to illuminate the figure and Dr. Reid gasped, loud enough to be heard within the chorus of insects that resounded from the giant figure. It had the size and general shape of Grollman. He was now covered with an epidermis of bubbling life. Millions of noisesome insects—myriad flies, bees, wasps, beetles, hornets, mantises, crickets, virtually every type of insect Gary had ever seen—pulsated along the massive frame, forcing it to lumber forward, reach out with a hand encrusted by miniature life forms.

"God!" choked Dr. Reid, apparently oblivious to the open jar which he held in a shaking hand. If it were possible for that skull face to manage an expression of horror, the chemist accomplished it. Perhaps it was the manner in which his eyes grew wide with red veins appearing like webwork amid the whites.

The horror that had been Grollman regarded the man in the wheelchair. Then it extended an insect-coated hand to Dr. Reid, grasped the scientist's wrist,—the wrist of the hand clutching the jar of pheromone. Dr. Reid was speechless, eyes bulging, mouth still locked into an eternal skeleton grin. In desperation he tried to yank his arm free but succeeded only in spilling the contents of the jar onto himself.

Dr. Reid screamed as he saw the insects stir to awareness. Insects flew, crawled, leapt from the giant figure, leaving only a cleaned skeleton that shone in the radiance of the flashlight. And as the insects fled the jointed bones and spread across the shivering body of Dr. Ronald Reid, the skeleton crumpled into a heap against the shadowed floor.

CHAPTER SEVENTEEN

Gary hurried behind Karen's chair. Setting down the flashlight, he struggled with the tight knots that bound her. He could hear Dr. Reid shrieking, hear the insects buzzing and chirruping insanely, as the first knot began to slacken.

"Save me!" screeched Dr. Reid.

Gary looked up, saw the chemist's other hand attacked by wasps. Reid's fingers relaxed, letting the insectarium smash against the floor to release the always hungry dermestid beetles. The detective remembered what he had seen them do to the iguana, then returned to Karen's ropes.

"Hurry—" she said.

Gary cast off the last of the ropes, freeing her.

Grabbing her assuringly, Gary looked back to Dr. Reid.

"Rutledge!" he screamed, arms flashing about to smash more jars of pheromone, more insectariums of irate life. "I can't stop what I'm doing! These God damned insects are forcing me to—'' But the tiger beetles that crowded into the doctor's mouth would not let him finish.

Gary and Karen watched as the insects moved away from them, leaving a vacant area on the floor in one corner of the room. Holding her, turning her face against his chest, the detective watched as Reid's hands jerked like those of an insect-covered puppet, grasped the tires of his wheelchair and forced it to roll forward. Choking, bleeding, Dr. Reid wheeled past the separated bones of his servant and out the laboratory door. Gary saw him rumble through the darkness of the anteroom and disappear around the corner.

The other insects in the laboratory followed.

Gary angled his flashlight toward the floor. There were only a few insects—grasshoppers and beetles, primarily—still in the room, except for those still imprisoned in Reid's insectariums. The detective bringing Karen with him stepped forward and the insects granted them passage.

Outside, Gary and Karen stood on the creaking floorboards beneath the eaves of the mansion. Karen pressed close against him as they both saw Dr. Reid roll across the sphagnum, leaving tracks over which the bog vapors soon settled.

There was nothing Gary could do for the chemist, even if he wanted to; the insects had seen to that, covering the doctor like a living suit of clothing until no part of his yet-living body showed through their congested numbers.

Still the wheelchair rolled. The black pit, which had already accepted one victim of the insects, gaped in its path. And in another moment the wheelchair, with its writhing insect covered figure, plunged headlong into fatal darkness.

But that was not all that Gary and Karen saw. For a melanoid tide was sweeping across the bog, comprised of so many miniscule creatures that their total forces were like the thickest smoke. They brushed over land, lashed through misty air, until they too were sucked into the darkness of the pit. At last a final muffled scream issued from the hole in the ground and faded amid the overpowering cacophony of the insects.

Gary and Karen waited. The detective did not look at his watch and forgot the time, a half hour, perhaps—or an hour. Then they detected new activity.

Flies were the first to emerge from the pit. Then came the other flying creatures, followed by beetles and mantises and their crusty ilk. When no more insects were seen to leave that yawning circle of blackness, Gary took Karen by the hand and wanly approached the edge of the pit. As his flash showed a legless skeleton upon which there was not the slightest evidence of flesh, Gary suspected that the night's horror had ended. He knew he was right when the tide of insects flowed back into the shadows of the bog or flew away with the nighttime wind.

"It's over," he told Karen, "I don't know how, but somehow those insects must have known that Reid was their enemy. They singled him out and had their revenge."

She held him firmly, face against his chest.

"Come on," he said, turning away from her and looking up at the smoking chimney of the mansion. He began to walk toward the house.

"Gary, what now?" she asked. "Why are we going back there?" Karen wriggled her shoulders as a vapory wind began to blow. She rubbed her arms with her hands as she almost ran to match Gary's pace.

But Gary did not answer her question; he almost did not hear her, so intent was he on the words once spoken to him by a gray-haired entomologist.

When they had reached the first anteroom, which still smelled and sounded of insect life, Gary replaced the fuses and brought light back to shine on the countless jars and insectariums that were still intact.

"Why did we come back?" she asked, still massaging her arms and shivering from the cold.

At last Gary spoke. "I said it was all over, Karen. But I was wrong. It's not over yet."

"Not over?"

Gary shook his head. "We have a chance to do something great tonight. Great, on a global scale."

"I don't understand."

"Think back, Hon," he said, holding her in an effort to give warmth, "back to that day we went to the museum. Back to what Ankrum told us about pheromone warfare, as he called it. Think of all the monstrous weapons of war that already plague the world, Karen. Germ warfare. Gas. Atomic bombs. And now this. Sure, synthetic pheromones might someday be used to curb insect pests, to benefit mankind. But we still can't take the chance that these advanced pheromones might fall into the possession of some hostile foreign power. It's just too great a risk."

"Then, you mean we'll have to get rid of them?"

"Exactly!" exclaimed Gary, letting go of Karen and scrutinizing the room. "We've got to give this place a thorough search. Find every scrap of information Reid had written—every journal, every diary, every formula, every scribbled note—that tells how he did his experiments. Then we'll gather up every pheromone jar in the house and get rid of them once and for all."

"How?" she asked.

"There's a chimney on this house. I'd bet that if we look down in the basement we'll find a coal furnace."

Together, Gary and Karen searched the anterooms and the laboratory. Dr. Reid had been systematic in recording his experiments. His journals were promptly discovered in a metal filing cabinet in one corner of the laboratory. A thorough inspection of the premises uncovered no other papers of any value.

In the basement, the old-fashioned coal burner provided not only warmth, but a means for Gary to dispose of the secrets that had caused the deaths of eight human beings and nearly killed two more. Opening the furnace, Gary discovered a good fire going.

Dr. Reid's papers—his notebooks with theories and formulae and the procedures and results of his experiments—were the first to feed the hot coal furnace. For brief moments, the papers seemed on the verge of snuffing out the fire, producing black smoke that rose through the chimney. But the cardboard cover of the bottom notebook was already starting to be burnt.

As the papers showed the first of their dancing flames, Gary began slowly to throw in the first jars of pheromones, each addition causing steam to hiss and spit on the hot coal.

When the last jar had been tossed into the furnace, Gary Rutledge stooped down for a final look at the deadly chemicals. Heat, ashes, steam and a foul smell.

Then he stepped away from the furnace door.

"Now it's really over," he told Karen, confidently. He felt as if his spirit and body were aglow to compete with the brilliance of the furnace. "The fire will destroy the pheromones for good."

"Thank God!"

At last Gary was free to look at Karen. Her face was smudged from the soot of the basement and furnace. She was enticing, even in torn clothes.

Gary clanged shut the furnace door. They kissed for a long time in the warmth of the heating furnace. And when they parted, both were smiling.

The first hints of dawn illuminated the sky above the colonial mansion. The sky was still overcast. And though the sun tried its best to shine upon the bog that morning, the thick gray clouds were obstructive. There was additional hindrance to the light in the form of dense smoke that puffed from the chimney.

Still, several beams of sunlight burst through the clouds and smoke to shine, however briefly, on the white Corvette that sped away from the mansion and back toward civilization.

CHAPTER EIGHTEEN

The Call goes out to all this day. Yet the Call is not identical. And those who receive the Call are not as before.

Cincidella stirs beneath a dry leaf. He crawls from his place of concealment and accepts the myriad feelings that he knows must be his. And though he hungers for that which the Way had once forbidden, he is no longer repulsed. On the contrary, Cincidella welcomes the hunger. Accepts it. Anticipates it.

His brothers also stir. Also hunger and hate and feel and know. They wonder when they shall march. And their master tells them that now they wait.

Mantis also knows and moves, stirred by cravings that fill his spirit with ambition. Mantis. And Grillus and Eciton and the others.

In the world of the bog, Cincidella lifts his head toward the gray-bright heavens, not to see some orblike God but rather to welcome the settling black cloud.

Soon, Cincidella knows, they will begin their march.

Soon . . .

For now there is no Call. The Call is now the Way. And the Way is theirs.

Cincidella waits.

For what he waits Cincidella only begins to know. Yet soon the knowledge will come to him. And this time it shall be different.